Pressed for Time

A Southern Quilting Mystery, Volume 8

Elizabeth Craig

Published by Elizabeth Craig, 2017.

PRESSED FOR TIME

First edition. September 11, 2017.

ISBN: 978-1946227027

Written by Elizabeth Craig.

For Mama and Daddy

Chapter One

Beatrice grinned at her fiancé, Wyatt. They were both reading in Beatrice's cozy cottage living room, but Beatrice decided to break the silence for a few minutes. "I'm so glad we decided on a small wedding. I can barely handle the fanfare involved in this one. It would have been even crazier if it were a large one."

Their wedding was now two weeks away. They'd decided on a chapel wedding with close friends and family invited. Piper, Beatrice's daughter, would be Beatrice's only attendant. It was the second wedding for both; each were widowed years before.

Wyatt smiled back at her, eyes crinkling. "Fanfare? You mean all the dinners, picnics, lunches, and barbeques in our honor? Everyone wants to wish us well, even if they can't all come to the ceremony or reception. It just means we're popular."

Beatrice snorted. "It just means *you're* popular. As minister, everyone knows you and loves you. I'm just part of the package."

"They're just happy that we're happy," said Wyatt, giving Beatrice's hand a squeeze.

They sat for a couple of minutes, enjoying the quiet of Beatrice's living room.

Beatrice said, "What's next on the list? I know we have something tonight, but I'm ashamed to say that I can't even remember what it is. The pre-wedding parties are becoming one big blur."

"We'll be at a dinner at Caspian Nelms's house," said Wyatt. He gave her a sideways look, anticipating what she was going to say.

Beatrice gave a gusty sigh. "At least I'll be with you. It'll be more bearable that way. And I'll have my party manners on—I know that Caspian is a friend of yours. He can just be a very difficult man."

"He can actually be rather kind, once you get to know him. I wouldn't say that he and I are very *close* friends, but we grew closer when he became more involved in the church. When I first started serving at the church, Caspian looked as if he wasn't very pleased that I was there. I worked hard to win him over," said Wyatt.

Beatrice said, "Somehow, when I see him, he always reminds me of Orson Welles's character in *Citizen Kane*."

"I don't think Caspian's house is quite as big. Or as empty," said Wyatt, smiling at her.

"And he's not nearly as wealthy. But he's still very, very wealthy," said Beatrice. "And somehow he never looks all that happy to me."

"I think he struggles with family stress," said Wyatt.

Beatrice didn't ask any more about that. She knew that Wyatt kept ministerial information to himself.

Wyatt continued lightly, "At least Meadow and Ramsay will be there."

Meadow and Ramsay were Beatrice's neighbors and friends. Ramsay was the chief of police and Meadow was very involved in their quilting guild, the Village Quilters. Meadow also had a habit of dragging Beatrice into lots of volunteering and quilting-related activities, which could be trying for Beatrice. Luckily, as plans for the wedding had gotten into full-swing, Meadow had backed off and instead had played a supportive role for her friend.

"That's true. I wish Piper could have made it, but she's been to everything else and now she's got some work to catch up on. And I'll try to meet more people at the party. You know so many people in this town ... maybe *everybody* in this town ... and I have a long way to go. But if I get overwhelmed, I'll hang out with Meadow at the drinks table," said Beatrice.

Wyatt said, "Just do what makes you feel comfortable." He smiled again at her and closed his book. "And now I think I should head back home and give us both the chance to rest before going out this evening."

"I know I should be resting. There's been this dog that has been barking day and night at some neighbor's house through the woods. I don't think I've been able to rest for days," said Beatrice.

"Have you tried earplugs?" asked Wyatt.

"I'm not so much a fan of earplugs," said Beatrice.

Wyatt said, "I wonder if something is wrong with the dog. Maybe we should go check on it."

"What's wrong with the dog is that the owner isn't doing a good job taking care of it," said Beatrice. She made a face at the cross note in her voice. "Sorry. The lack of sleep is rearing its ugly head. And you're right—I'll make a note to try to run over there and see what's going on with the dog. But in the meantime, I have a feeling that my resting this afternoon will involve a brisk walk with Noo-Noo," said Beatrice.

Wyatt grinned as the little corgi pricked up her ears at the words *walk* and *Noo-Noo*.

Beatrice said, "I'm feeling way too restless to rest. Or maybe the reading time was my version of rest today."

"What are you tackling now?" asked Wyatt, squinting at Beatrice's book's cover. "It's a massive book, whatever it is."

"It's something Ramsay let me borrow. You know how he's always giving me book recommendations. It's *Moby Dick*." Beatrice sighed. "I think some of the pages are commentary. At least I hope they are. Otherwise, this novel is entirely too long."

"Haven't you read it before?" asked Wyatt. "Maybe for school?"

"Oh, I read it in school. I didn't care for it then and I thought maybe I'd like it better or understand it better at this point in my life," said Beatrice. "I was looking at Ramsay's bookcase and said as much to him, and the next thing I knew, I was taking *Moby Dick* back home with me."

"What do you think?" asked Wyatt.

"I think that there are far too many descriptions of harpoons. But I do like it better than I did in school," said Beatrice. "Still, part of me wishes that I was reading something a little *lighter*. I mean ... *Moby Dick*? Right before one's wedding? I could use more of an escape."

Wyatt reached down to pet Noo-noo. "You'd rather not be escaping to a 19th century Nantucket whaling ship?"

Beatrice tilted her head to one side. "Either you have a frighteningly good memory, or else you've read *Moby Dick* a lot more recently than I have."

"Maybe a little bit of both?" said Wyatt, a twinkle in his eye. "All right. I'll pick you up at six? How does that sound?"

"It sounds like I need to start seriously thinking about what to wear tonight," said Beatrice.

After Wyatt left, Beatrice surveyed her closet with Noo-noo helping. She seriously needed to get some dry cleaning done. She'd tried to look nice, even for the barbeques. Now she either needed to decide to go more casual, buy more clothes, or go to the dry cleaner. Going more casual was sounding most appealing of the group.

But she couldn't do that tonight. She didn't know a lot about Caspian Nelms, but she knew enough to realize that tonight wasn't going to be a lively, casual event. After a few minutes of deep thought, she decided to go very basic. She pulled out a pair of black slacks, a white blouse, and a strand of pearls and matching pearl earrings. The black and white look usually complemented Beatrice's height and her bob of silvery hair that layered around her face.

With this chore out of the way, Beatrice asked Noo-noo, "Want to go for a walk?"

The corgi tilted her head, listening intently to Beatrice, before giving a joyful woof in reply. Beatrice grabbed Noo-noo's leash. The little dog bounced around, grinning at Beatrice before sitting obediently still to have her harness put on.

She first walked through the woods and toward the sound of the dog's barking. It was a small house up on the hill. Noo-noo perked up her ears as if tuning in to what the dog was saying. By the time they were close enough to see the dog, it was excitedly putting its paws up on the chain link fence and looking soulfully at them.

The dog was fairly large—maybe a mix of a golden retriever and a collie of some sort. As soon as Beatrice drew closer, he flopped to his back. His eyes seemed to be trying to tell Beatrice something.

"Are you out here all day and all night?" fussed Beatrice. She reached a hand tentatively through the fence and rubbed the dog's tummy. He quickly jumped back up and rubbed his head against her hand.

"You're a friendly guy, that's for sure," said Beatrice. "I'll knock on the door and see what I can find out."

But when Beatrice walked around to the front of the little house, there was no car in the driveway and no answer when she knocked at the door. She hesitated. The dog definitely was well-fed. And he had what appeared to be fresh water in the yard, too. She decided to come back another time to try to talk to the owner again.

Beatrice set off in the direction of town instead of the direction of Meadow's and Ramsay's house. She'd see them both later and Beatrice didn't want to be waylaid by Meadow. It seemed that whenever she walked by Meadow's house, Meadow was either on her way in or out of the refurbished barn that served as her home. And, whenever Meadow spotted her, she'd immediately hijack her walk (talking non-stop the whole way), strong-arm her into her house, and feed her. It was the feeding that Beatrice especially wanted to avoid. If she kept eating extra meals in addition to all the party food, those black slacks wouldn't fit for very long.

Beatrice set a brisk pace, keeping those extra calories in mind. She heard a loud engine coming and hopped off the road, pulling Noo-noo with her. Sure enough, Miss Sissy's large, decrepit old Lincoln roared toward them, veering recklessly off the road as the old woman shook an arthritic fist out the window at Beatrice. "Road hog!" yelled Miss Sissy from the car.

Beatrice, completely unfazed by this encounter since it happened weekly, continued on her walk with the equally unfazed Noo-noo.

They passed the old-timey grocery store built from old gray stones with ivy climbing up the side. A couple of good old boys were telling tales in rocking chairs in the front. Beatrice lifted a hand, waving at them as they passed. Next to it was the full-service gas station where there were still attendants in uniform—more good-old-boys. These boys were in their seventies and apparently had no intention of stopping). Noo-noo and Beatrice kept up their quick pace past little art galleries, a bookstore, an ice cream parlor, and a boutique.

When they reached the outside of the bakery and cake shop, Beatrice paused. June Bug, the owner and baker, was busily locking up with keys in one hand, a large cake in a container in the other. Beatrice glanced at her watch. Sure enough, it was after five o'clock. She and Noo-noo were going to have to hurry back.

June Bug's brow was creased and she looked distracted, as though she had something on her mind. But she beamed as she saw Beatrice and set down the container and bent to rub Noo-noo's tummy, since the corgi had immediately flopped over on her back for a tummy rub. The little woman straightened up to her full, diminutive height and smiled at her friend again. "Getting ready for the big day?"

Beatrice nodded. "And how! I think my life will be a lot quieter after all the pre-wedding festivities are over. One of the highlights of my wedding day will be an exclusive June Bug cake."

June Bug's round face flushed with pleasure. "I'll work hard on it." She stood back up and Noo-noo stood up too, grinning at the little woman.

"June Bug, all you *do* is work hard. It'll be wonderful to enjoy a wedding cake that tastes as good as it looks, for once," said Beatrice. "But tell me about *you*. I've been so busy lately that I haven't seen you for a while. And a couple of days ago, I thought I saw the shop closed during the day. How have you been?"

June Bug's smile faded and she blinked rapidly. Beatrice was startled to see a single tear fall down her cheek.

"Oh! I'm so sorry," said June Bug, blushing. But she couldn't seem to stop other tears from following the first.

"No, I'm sorry," said Beatrice, dismayed. "Something's wrong and I had no idea. What is it?"

June Bug managed to speak after a few moments of trying to compose herself. "It's my sister. Younger sister."

Beatrice said, "Somehow, I didn't even realize you had a sister."

"She moved away years ago and we didn't get to visit much. Not as much as we should have!" June Bug's voice choked again with tears.

Beatrice put her hand on June Bug's back. "And something happened? Is that it?"

June Bug nodded miserably, eyes focused stubbornly on the sidewalk below her feet. "Car accident," she murmured.

"I'm so sorry, June Bug," said Beatrice. "I had no idea."

The little woman gave her a small smile. "I haven't told anyone," she said in her soft voice. "I just closed the shop for a couple of days. My aunt arranged a small memorial service for my sister. And then there's Katy."

"Katy?" asked Beatrice.

"My niece," said June Bug softly.

Beatrice was now straining to hear her. "Wait. So—is your niece is staying with you?"

June Bug nodded. "Katy never knew her father and I didn't ask my sister about him." Her face pinched with worry. "I hope I can do a good job. I don't know much about children."

"But you know how to love them," said Beatrice warmly. "And that's all that matters. You're going to do a great job. How old is Katy?"

"She's eight years old," said June Bug. "She's with a sitter right now, but I'm thinking that tomorrow I'll take her to the shop with me."

Beatrice said, "That's a great age, June Bug. And what's more, Piper can show her around her school! Piper teaches second grade at the elementary school and I bet that Katy is probably in that grade. And you have so much energy, you'll be easily able to keep up with an eight-year-old."

June Bug beamed at her, although there was still a kernel of worry in her eyes. She glanced at her watch. "Oops, got to run. This cake has to be delivered before I run back home." She paused and added shyly in a rush, "Do you have something old? For the ceremony, I mean?"

Beatrice gave a short laugh. "You know, I don't think I've even thought that far ahead! No, I don't have something old."

June Bug flushed again happily, smiled at Beatrice, and quickly trotted off.

Beatrice and Noo-noo hurried back home and Beatrice quickly got ready for Caspian's dinner party. She was just putting on a pair of black shoes when Wyatt arrived to pick her up.

Ten minutes later, Wyatt was parking in a circular driveway in front of a two-story gray stone house. Although *house* wasn't really the word to describe it. It was a looming mansion. In theory, it should be pretty—the stone was pretty and the ironwork on the door and the matching ironwork of the balconies outside some of the windows was pretty—but the house itself had a very sullen appearance. Beatrice shivered.

Wyatt frowned in concern. "Everything all right? Should I drive you back home and tell them you aren't feeling well? We *have* been doing a lot."

"No, no. I'm fine. It's just my over-active imagination getting wound up over nothing. The house has this sort of gothic edge to it, that's all," said Beatrice, feeling silly.

"I know what you mean. But the grounds are beautiful. Caspian has a full-time gardener, Barkis," said Wyatt as they got out of the car.

"Barkis. Straight from *David Copperfield*. Is that his first name or his last name?" asked Beatrice.

Wyatt shrugged. "Who knows?" he said with a chuckle. "He must be eighty years old if he's a day and he's been here his entire life."

Beatrice saw an old man with a hunched back and beard walking with a pair of hedge trimmers. "That's him, I'm guessing?"

"It is. Hi, Barkis!" called out Wyatt.

Barkis squinted at him, grunted, and continued with his business.

"Friendly fellow," said Beatrice under her breath. "Is he possibly related to Miss Sissy?"

"At least he didn't shake a fist at us," said Wyatt, unfazed. As minister, he possessed a lot more generosity of spirit than Beatrice had.

They used the heavy iron door knocker to pound on the equally-heavy wooden door. No one came.

"Are we sure we got the date and time right?" asked Beatrice.

Before Wyatt could answer, the door creaked open. A thin man in his forties opened the door with a dour look on his face. He saw Beatrice and raised his eyebrows. This made Beatrice want to check to see if she somehow spilled something on her white blouse.

Wyatt seemed to know who the unwelcoming man was. "Hawkins! So good to see you. Is your father doing well?"

Hawkins was apparently Caspian's son. He shrugged. "I suppose so."

A booming voice behind Hawkins made him wince. "Hawkins? Haven't you ever answered a door before? The idea is to let the guests *in*."

Sarcasm dripped through the man's voice.

"Yes, Father," said Hawkins in a tight voice. He reluctantly opened the door wider, letting Beatrice and Wyatt inside.

Chapter Two

It took Beatrice a moment to adjust to the dim lighting inside the house, which was even dimmer than the fading light outside. Hawkins had quickly walked away in the direction of a large living room. Actually, Beatrice supposed, it was more of an old-fashioned drawing room. It was long, right by the entrance, and didn't look like the type of room that anyone would choose to relax in. It appeared to exist purely for entertaining. There was a grand piano at one end, a mural on the ceiling, expensive-looking vases on pedestals in the corners, and gold-leaf covered chairs and settees scattered throughout.

Beatrice turned to Caspian, who was wryly surveying her. He clutched a nearly-empty highball glass and wore a suit with a tightly-knotted tie. Despite his eighty years, he looked hale and hearty and loomed over everyone at his height, which must be over six and a half feet. His smile and eyes were cold. "What a lovely room," Beatrice said.

He grunted. But then he extended his hand to her, "Good to see you, Beatrice."

Beatrice shook his hand. "Thanks for inviting us."

"You're very lucky, marrying this fellow," he said brusquely, no sense of humor evident in his declaration.

Beatrice said, "I'd agree with that."

Wyatt said lightly, "I think the opposite is true. At any rate, we're getting excited about the big day."

Caspian drained the drink. Then he seemed to realize his guests were empty-handed. "You'll want a drink," he said decidedly. He glanced around. "Where's that girl? Where'd she run off to?"

A wry voice from the corner of the room said, "If you're referring to me, I'm here. Although, I'm hardly a girl."

A middle-aged woman stood. She was attractive in a hard way and wore a good deal of eye makeup.

"Well, come on over and play hostess," said Caspian.

The woman walked over to them and smiled at Wyatt. To Beatrice she reached out a hand and said, "You must be Beatrice. I'm Sadie Bryant, Caspian's daughter."

Before Beatrice could say that it was nice to meet her, she walked off to the drinks table. "Bourbon and coke? Vodka and tonic? Gin and tonic?" she called. She weaved almost imperceptibly on her high heels and Beatrice wondered if she'd already had a couple of beverages, herself.

Caspian gave a raspy chuckle. "I gather that Wyatt isn't so fond of the hard stuff. Maybe a beer for Wyatt?"

"That would be perfect," said Wyatt with a smile.

Beatrice said, "I'll have a vodka tonic, please."

Caspian shook his glass. "And I'll have a refresher."

A few minutes later, they were seated in a small conversation area of gilded chairs. Caspian's social skills were either rusty or weren't ever well-developed to begin with. His version of conversation was to interrogate Beatrice with a spate of questions about her background, her daughter, and her opinion on politics and other topics. The only thing he seemed interested in was Beatrice's experience as an art museum curator in Atlanta.

Beatrice relaxed a bit in relief as Caspian quickly jumped into conversation with Wyatt, chuckling from time to time at his stories and jokes. Beatrice was impressed again by Wyatt's ability to connect with anybody, anywhere. She definitely didn't have that gift.

Beatrice decided to amuse herself by observing the other people in the room. Caspian's son, Hawkins, was moodily staring at his father and his sister. From time to time he got up, left the room, and returned with a full glass. She supposed that he didn't want his speedy refills observed and commented on by his father. But she suspected that Caspian didn't miss much.

Hawkins's drinking certainly wasn't lost on his sister. She leveled a glare at him after his latest refill. "Really?" she asked him under her breath.

He ignored her.

Sadie said in a scolding voice, "Maybe your disposition would improve if you actually made an effort to share your life with someone. Like Wynona. Although she was too good for you."

Hawkins took this opportunity to get up and leave the room again. Sadie stared broodingly at the floor. Beatrice shifted uncomfortably on the gilded armchair.

Wyatt's and Caspian's conversation wrapped up and then it really got quiet in the room. Sadie stood up swiftly. "I should check with the caterer and make sure dinner is ready."

There was a knock at the front door and Beatrice jumped up with alacrity. "I'll get it," she said.

She opened the door to see her friend Meadow and Meadow's husband, Ramsay there. "Thank heavens you're here," hissed Beatrice.

Meadow beamed at her through her red-framed glasses. "Good to see you, too!" Meadow had apparently decided not to take the occasion to dress more conventionally than she usually did. She wore a bright, multicolored skirt in loud oranges and reds and purples with a black top. Her long gray braid did have a festive purple bow at the bottom in acknowledgement that this was a celebration.

In usual Meadow fashion, she immediately walked in and drew attention to the atmosphere inside. "Hey, it's too quiet in here. It's time to celebrate, remember? Woo-hoo! Wyatt and Beatrice!"

Caspian Nelms was staring at Meadow as if she were an alien who'd landed at his house. He set his drink down and walked slowly forward to greet Meadow and Ramsay. Perhaps he was thinking that he couldn't remember having invited her. As a matter of fact, Beatrice recalled, he likely *hadn't* invited her. She seemed to remember that Meadow said that Sadie had extended the invitation. At least the dead silence and the strange hostility in the house was coming to a close. Meadow would call them out on it, otherwise.

Sadie, hearing Meadow's voice, quickly reappeared. She looked genuinely pleased to see her. Even Hawkins stood up to greet them.

Meadow seemed too keyed up to sit down. "Sadie, didn't you say that there were some old quilts here from generations ago? I'd love to see those." Her eyes danced. "And see the rest of this gorgeous mansion."

Ramsay rolled his eyes, although he was used to Meadow's antics.

Sadie, who still seemed eager to get away from the tense atmosphere in the drawing room, said, "I can give you the grand tour. But first, let's get you some drinks."

"I'd like one more, as well," said her father.

The next few minutes were spent with both Sadie and Hawkins going back and forth from the drinks table to the kitchen to help the caterer bring out the hors d'oeuvres. Beatrice spotted what looked like a pâté with apricots and a vegetable tart.

"It might be easier to eat when we come back from the tour," said Sadie. She looked at her brother through narrowed eyes. "Hawkins, you can come with us."

It was clearly not a suggestion, but a command. Hawkins reluctantly followed them. Caspian said, "I'm going to put my feet up for twenty-winks before the meal. Wake me when you're ready for dinner."

Sadie frowned. "But you'll miss the hors d'oeuvres."

Caspian was already heading away.

Sadie muttered, "He's always slipping away for a nap. Sorry about that." She gave them an apologetic look. "This probably wasn't what you thought you were signing up for. Father has never been great at making conversation or giving parties. But he likes Wyatt so much that he thought he'd make an exception."

Meadow said, "And who *wouldn't* like Wyatt? He's immensely likeable."

"Don't worry about your father," said Beatrice. "Taking naps when you want to is a privilege of age."

"Now show us the rest of this gorgeous house!" said Meadow.

Sadie looked at her watch. "All right. The other guests should be coming in around the time that we're done."

Meadow asked, "And where are Malcolm and Della?"

Hawkins said gloomily, "They're hiding somewhere in the house."

Sadie gave him an irritated look. "They're not *hiding*. Malcolm is chronically late and Della arrived just minutes before Beatrice and Wyatt did. They should be out soon." Her voice implied bad things would happen if they didn't.

Sadie started walking down a hall lined with portraits of annoyed-looking ancestors in fancy dress.

Beatrice murmured to Wyatt, "Remind me who Malcolm and Della are?"

"Malcolm is Caspian's younger son and Della is his girlfriend," whispered Wyatt. "I believe Della lives here."

"Hope they're a bit livelier than everyone else here," said Beatrice under her breath.

Sadie gave a good tour of the large home. There were sitting areas, a conservatory, a ballroom, a library, and many bedrooms. Each room was filled with dark-wood antiques, gilded furniture, grandfather clocks, and rather musty drapes. There were some beautiful old quilts along the way. Hawkins did manage to slip unobtrusively away during the tour, although Beatrice and Ramsay both noticed.

Sadie was pointing out a large portrait of a rather haughty-looking ancestor at the top of the marble staircase when Beatrice heard a noise downstairs. She glanced down to see the bearded Barkis downstairs, still holding hedge clippers. Beatrice gave him a half-hearted wave and he glowered back at her.

Sadie was nearly done with the tour when a handsome man of middle-age appeared. His elegant dress and ultra-groomed appearance reminded Beatrice of some of the older male movie stars. He gave an apologetic grin, showing off his perfect teeth. "Sorry to be late." He reached forward to shake Beatrice's hand with a firm grip. "I'm Malcolm Nelms. This is my girlfriend, Della."

He motioned to a cute girl behind him with long brown hair, dimples, and a cheery smile. She bounced forward to shake their hands. "I'm Della."

"I think we know everyone else, don't we, Della?" Malcolm asked lightly.

Della beamed at them all. "We seem to! Hi, Wyatt! Hi, Meadow and Ramsay."

Sadie said crisply, "Since you're finally done getting ready, you can finish giving them the tour. I'm going to go check in with the kitchen and get ready to greet the other guests." She glanced around. "And round up Hawkins," she added through gritted teeth.

Malcolm said, "Let's see. Looks like you haven't seen the music room yet. We'll head that way and then wrap up and head back to the drawing room. Where's Father?" he asked. "Wasn't up for the grand tour?"

"No, he's taking a short nap before supper," said Wyatt. "I think we might have worn him out a little."

"*Everything* seems to wear him out these days," said Malcolm. "At least he's lying down. He'll be in better humor for dinner that way."

Della said gushingly to Beatrice, "Tell me all about your wedding plans!"

During the next ten minutes, they saw the music room, talked about the upcoming wedding (while Ramsay kept glancing at his watch), and finally walked back to the drawing room.

Hawkins was there, looking somewhat bleary-eyed. Beatrice suspected that he'd had another drink after he'd left the tour of the home. Sadie hadn't returned from the kitchen yet. There was a knock at the front door and Malcolm opened it to greet more guests.

Soon the atmosphere in the house was much brighter, with the influx of ten or twelve more guests.

Beatrice sidled over to Ramsay. "You're looking cheerier."

"Well, it's finally more of a party, isn't it?" he said ruefully. "I'd been feeling very sorry for myself for not being at home reading a good book for the last thirty or forty-five minutes. No offence, Beatrice—I know it's a party for you and Wyatt."

"No, I'd agree," she said. She frowned, glancing at her watch. "Don't you think someone should be getting Caspian up? Surely he wants a few minutes to wake up before it's time to eat."

Ramsay made a face. "Having Caspian around will hardly improve the atmosphere. I don't think he's ever taken a liking to me. And he seems to break out in hives around Meadow."

Beatrice glanced across the room. "Regardless, it looks as if someone is finally going to wake him up."

Sadie indeed seemed to be squaring her shoulders in anticipation of the task as she left the room and headed toward the stairs. But it really was getting time to eat, despite all the heavy hors d'oeuvres. Beatrice was starting to get sleepy and was ready to have her dinner, say her thank yous, and turn in for the night.

A few minutes later, Sadie returned, face white. She glanced around the room until her gaze lit on Ramsay.

Beatrice reached across and laid a hand on Ramsay's arm. "Sadie needs you," she said quietly. She felt a cold shiver up her spine, although she didn't really know what had happened.

Ramsay took one look at Sadie's face and stood swiftly up, following her out of the drawing room while everyone continued their increasingly loud conversations.

Wyatt exchanged a look with Beatrice. "What do you think that's about?" he murmured.

"Maybe Caspian has taken ill," said Beatrice. But even as she said the words, she didn't fully believe them.

Ramsay returned with Sadie a minute later. Looking swiftly around the room, he leaned over and murmured in the ears of Hawkins and Malcolm. They stood, looking serious, and Malcolm motioned Della to join him.

The next time Ramsay returned to the group, he was alone. He raised his voice to speak over the party chatter. "If I could have your attention? Unfortunately, there's been a tragedy. I will brief everyone soon, but for now, I need you all to head out to the driveway. And I'll need you to stay on the grounds until after I've spoken to each of you."

The guests murmured to each other in concern as they filed out of the house. They saw the family huddled together, some distance away from the house. No one approached them.

Meadow said to Beatrice in an uneasy voice, "Caspian must be dead for Ramsay to ask us to leave the house."

"Dead, or murdered?" asked Beatrice quietly. "Surely Ramsay wouldn't behave this way over a natural death."

Wyatt said, "Maybe he's not sure and he's trying to be as careful as possible."

A good deal of time went by. Most of the guests were sitting in their cars with their air conditioning running. Meadow sat with Wyatt and Beatrice in their car. At one point, a state police car pulled up. Ramsay was walking around getting statements.

Meadow said, "This is going to go faster than it looks. Most of these folks hadn't even arrived at the party by the time Caspian left to take his nap."

Beatrice said, "I think you're right. Ramsay's heading this way now."

Ramsay hopped into the back of the van.

Meadow demanded, "Ramsay, what on earth is going on? Did something happen to Caspian?"

"He's dead," said Ramsay quietly.

Chapter Three

"Well, that's what we were all guessing. But you usually don't herd people around and question them over natural deaths. Didn't Caspian simply die in his sleep?" asked Meadow.

Ramsay said grimly, "I don't think so. I can't be sure, but I think his death was made to look that way. I believe he might have been smothered by a pillow." He paused and then asked them, "Did you notice anything unusual about his eyes?"

Beatrice thought about this. She'd noticed him rolling his eyes at Meadow and noticed the cold looks he gave his children. But she didn't notice anything specific about them. She shook her head slowly and Meadow and Wyatt did, too.

"They weren't especially bloodshot?" asked Ramsay.

"No, I'd have noticed that," said Beatrice.

"The pathologist will need to see if he has high levels of carbon dioxide in his blood," said Ramsay. Then he sighed. "And I believe he will."

Meadow said, "This is a first, Ramsay. Usually you're not on the scene of the crime when it actually happens."

"It's pretty brazen to commit murder with the local police chief in the house," agreed Beatrice.

Ramsay asked, "In case I missed anything, who did you notice leave the rest of the group while we were there?"

Meadow snorted. "Everybody. Nobody stayed in the group the whole time. Della and Malcolm weren't even *part* of the group until late."

Ramsay said thoughtfully, "That's true. I didn't think of that. So, technically, one or both of them could have smothered Caspian before joining us."

Wyatt said, "Unfortunately, I also saw both Hawkins and Sadie leave the group from time to time." He quickly added, "But I think they were both checking on the kitchen and maybe refilling their drinks."

Meadow exclaimed, "How could their children do such a thing? He was their father. And at a special occasion for our Wyatt and Beatrice!"

"He also didn't seem to be on great terms with some of his children," said Beatrice dryly.

Ramsay looked encouragingly at Beatrice. "What did you notice?"

"Well, Sadie was generally short with him. I think she was exasperated by his taking a nap during the party. And Hawkins seemed very tense around his father. I'm sure that's why he was refilling his drink so much."

Ramsay sighed. "So they all left the group and at least two of his children appeared to be at odds with their father in some way."

Wyatt said, "At least Malcolm seemed to be in a good humor."

"But he wasn't around his father at all, so that might have put him in a better mood," said Beatrice.

Ramsay nodded and snapped shut the small notebook he'd been making notes in. "All right. Thanks, y'all. You're free to leave now."

He walked off to speak with the state police.

Meadow said, "Wyatt, could you take me home? I should leave the car for Ramsay or else he'll be walking back."

"Of course, I will," said Wyatt.

He drove out of the large, circular driveway and back out into the street.

Meadow gave a gusty sigh. "Now I'll have to go home and cook something since we didn't eat dinner and who knows what time Ramsay will make his way home."

"Why not just leave sandwich stuff out for him? We all ate a lot of hors d'oeuvres, after all. Don't worry about a full meal," said Beatrice.

Wyatt gave Beatrice a sympathetic smile, "It's not exactly what we expected tonight, was it?"

"No. Although it was just as uncomfortable as I thought it would be," said Beatrice.

Meadow, leaning forward from the backseat to look at Beatrice said, "Now you'll have something to keep your mind and your nerves off your upcoming wedding."

Beatrice blinked at Meadow. "Nerves? I don't think I had any nerves."

"Well, if you don't now, you soon will."

Beatrice said, "It's going by too quickly for me to have nerves. All the preparation and the festivities are sort of a blur. I hope I'm going to be able to remember details from the wedding and reception, but I have a feeling that it will be so busy that I'll just remember bits and pieces."

Meadow said, "Well, you never know. Nerves can crop up. This is the perfect distraction, although ... poor Caspian, of course," said Meadow, somewhat unconvincingly.

Beatrice said, "I did have one question. For some reason, I thought that Caspian lived alone in the house. But then, with all the family there, I wondered if they lived locally, or if they lived on the estate."

"Oh, goodness, they all live with their daddy. It's just like the old soap opera, *Dallas*. And probably as much *drama* as Dallas, too," said Meadow, rolling her eyes.

"And Della lives there, too?"

"For the time being, at least. But then, the place does have a ton of bedrooms, doesn't it? Della might even have her own room there, since she and Malcolm aren't married yet," said Meadow.

Beatrice wasn't at all sure that was the case, but allowed Meadow to assume the proprieties were being observed. "There must have been eight or nine bedrooms that I saw," she agreed.

Meadow said, "And since you didn't know anyone very well, I'd like to hear your first impressions of them."

Beatrice said ruefully, "I'm afraid I didn't exactly get a sterling impression of any of them. Although I'm willing to chalk that up to a somewhat stressful evening for the family."

"What was stressful about it?" demanded Meadow. "They were hosting a party with delicious foods they didn't even prepare. They had beverages at hand. They reside in a marvelous mansion with amazing artwork. I'd like that kind of stress, myself."

Wyatt said, "Sometimes parties *themselves* are stressful for some people. I think that's what Beatrice means."

"Pooh," said Meadow. "They shouldn't be so delicate. But go on, Beatrice. What were your impressions of them?"

Beatrice thought for a minute. "Caspian seemed to actively dislike his children."

Wyatt said sadly, "He's never seemed very happy. I was hoping that he could find some peace in his later years."

Meadow snorted. "Caspian brought a lot of that misery on himself. He should have tried building better relationships with his family."

"Caspian especially seemed at odds with Hawkins. And all Hawkins seemed to want to do was to escape his father and refresh his drink," said Beatrice.

Meadow nodded. "I think you're right. Of course, from what I've heard, there's definitely some back-story there. Something to do with Caspian being very stingy about his money and Hawkins wanting more of it. There has been gossip through the years." Then she snapped her fingers, as if remembering something.

"And something else?" asked Beatrice.

"A woman," said Meadow. "And not just any woman. Someone you know and have been working with very closely recently."

Beatrice, who was ready to get back home by now, sighed. "Meadow, I don't want to play guessing games now."

"Wynona Thigpen! Your florist for the wedding," said Meadow triumphantly.

Wyatt looked thoughtful. "I believe I did hear something about Wynona and the family."

"Yes! Because Wynona has been so mad that she's told everyone about it! That's why it's not even gossip," said Meadow.

Beatrice said, "What about Wynona?"

"Well, she was dating Hawkins. For quite a long time. And Hawkins wasn't at all like he was tonight. He was actually *happy*. He'd smile and laugh with her and just acted like a totally different person," said Meadow.

"I'm sensing a big 'but' here," said Beatrice.

"But Caspian didn't approve of the relationship," said Meadow. "And that was the end of that."

Beatrice frowned. "Didn't *approve* of it? But this isn't *Romeo and Juliet*. So what if he didn't approve? Hawkins is old enough to decide to date whomever he pleases. Way *past* that point, as a matter of fact."

"But there's money involved. And rumors that Hawkins was in debt. Hawkins sure wouldn't want to be cut out of Caspian's will. I'd heard that maybe he had all these gambling debts. I suppose he broke his gambling addiction—poor people can't gamble! Anyway, he broke things off with Wynona and she was furious. She'll talk about it at the drop of a hat, so be sure to mention it to her next time. Now what did you think of the others?" asked Meadow.

Wyatt said, "Aside from the others, I thought Malcolm and Della seemed very happy tonight."

"I did have a better impression of them," admitted Beatrice, "Although that's not really fair, since they weren't even with us the entire time. I should have had a *bad* impression because they were being bad hosts and letting Sadie and Hawkins take up the slack. And mostly Sadie."

Meadow said, "Della quilts!" in the tone of someone who has stated all that could possibly be said on a subject.

"That hardly absolves her of murder," noted Beatrice dryly. "However much you might want to believe the contrary."

"Oh, I know. But I think it does speak to her character a little. She's really just taken it up. She's spending tons of time in Posy's shop, getting fabric and notions and figuring it all out. Della asked me for tips! And even asked Miss Sissy," said Meadow. "I'm hoping to convince her to join the Village Quilters guild."

Beatrice had the feeling that this proved Della might be something of a flatterer. She moved on, "What about the long-suffering Sadie?" asked Beatrice. "She didn't seem to be enjoying herself tonight, but considering how busy she was, it's hardly any wonder."

Wyatt said, "I've been happy to see Sadie reconnect with her family. Especially her father."

"Reconnect?" asked Beatrice.

Meadow said, "They've been estranged. For years!"

"Over what?" asked Beatrice.

"I have no idea. But isn't it good that Sadie reached out to her father recently? *Especially* considering the tragic event tonight," said Meadow, clicking her tongue.

Beatrice said, "I'm glad she had the chance to make up with him before he died. Family is so important. Which reminds me—I needed to tell you about June Bug."

"What about June Bug?" asked Meadow.

"Her sister died in a car crash and June Bug's niece is now living with her. Katy, I think her name is. She's only eight years old," said Beatrice.

Meadow gasped and Wyatt said, "I hadn't heard about this—maybe the church can help her."

Beatrice said, "She hasn't told anyone about it, but she seemed sad and I pressed her on it. She has a sitter who's helping her out, but maybe there's a better way."

Wyatt said, "Once school starts, the church has an afterschool program that's been really popular. That might be a good solution for June Bug."

"But there's always the expense," said Meadow in a worried voice. "June Bug doesn't have a lot of extra money, even though the bakery is doing really well."

"The church has funds to offer scholarships to parents or guardians who might be in need," said Wyatt.

"I'll tell her about it," said Meadow. "And I want to meet Katy, too."

Beatrice said, "She's apparently planning on bringing her to the bakery some, so I'm sure you will."

Meadow's eyes lit up. "Maybe she can come to the next guild meeting! It's on a Saturday."

Beatrice said dryly, "Why do I have the feeling that Katy is going to end up as a quilter?"

Wyatt pulled up into Beatrice's driveway, which was on the way to Meadow's house. "See you soon, Beatrice. I expect I'll find out a lot more from Ramsay tonight, although it might be very late," said Meadow.

Beatrice said quickly, "Just catch me up on it tomorrow. I'm turning in as soon as possible."

Wyatt said with a smile, "We've had lots of celebrating lately. I think it might have worn Beatrice out."

Meadow said, "Oh, I bet. And just imagine how crazy it will be when our darlings Ash and Piper are married!"

After such a long day, Beatrice decidedly did *not* want to think about that. She was thrilled about her daughter marrying Meadow's son, but right now she'd rather not consider the events *surrounding* the wedding.

"Sleep well," said Wyatt with a small smile. Beatrice thought that sometimes he could read her mind.

"That's right. Sweet dreams!" said Meadow.

Beatrice had turned in concerned that she had too much on her mind to be able to sleep well. Plus, there was the barking dog to consider, and, right on cue, it was persistently barking. She made a mental note to try to connect with the owner again soon and turned on a fan to help combat the noise. To her surprise, she woke up with daylight streaming through her window after a full night's sleep.

As she lay in bed, though, she frowned. She felt as though something had awakened her, and she didn't think it was the sunshine. Beatrice lay still to listen for it again. Then she heard it: not only the persistently barking dog (which was fast becoming background noise), but a low growl from the other room.

Chapter Four

Beatrice quickly got out of bed, pulling her ruby-red robe around her and stuffing her feet into a nearby pair of slippers. But by the time she'd hurried from her bedroom, Noo-noo's growl turned into more of a surprised woof of recognition as the little dog stared through the back door from the living room into the backyard.

Beatrice followed her gaze and saw a particularly wild-looking Miss Sissy. The old woman was in the azalea bushes, small sticks and flowers sticking out of her hair. Her ancient floral dress was smeared with mud and she wore a scowl on her face. Had Miss Sissy finally lost what remained of her mind?

Beatrice quickly opened the back door. "Miss Sissy?" she asked in a cautious tone. "Why don't you come inside and sit for a few minutes?"

Miss Sissy stared blankly at her.

Beatrice continued, "I was just about to make some breakfast. How does eggs and bacon and hash browns sound?" She knew the old woman, despite her size, was a voracious eater. In fact, she could likely wipe out the remaining inventory of her kitchen pantry, given the chance.

Miss Sissy only blinked.

"I can throw in some toast and fruit, too," said Beatrice lightly.

The old woman's face crumpled, then she teared up and started crying in earnest.

Beatrice stood stock still, completely unaccustomed to an emotional Miss Sissy. Oh, she could be *emotional*, but the emotion was ordinarily limited to anger. She rushed out and carefully walked the old woman out of the middle of the azalea bushes, getting quite a few sticks and flowers on her red robe in the process.

"It's all right," said Beatrice. "Let's go inside. Everything will work itself out."

Miss Sissy obediently allowed herself to be led indoors. Noo-noo sniffed her in commiseration and the old woman started howling again, stooping over to hug the startled corgi, which looked at Beatrice with big eyes.

Beatrice wasn't sure what had happened because once Miss Sissy got inside, she clung to Noo-noo and wouldn't talk. Beatrice handed her a box of tissues and walked into the kitchen to deliver the meal she'd promised and to give Miss Sissy an opportunity to calm down and collect herself. Beatrice was already wondering if she should call Posy for help. Posy, her friend who owned the Patchwork Cottage quilt shop, always had a good way with Miss Sissy.

She'd almost finished scrambling the eggs and frying the bacon when a subdued Miss Sissy croaked, "Wyatt."

"Wyatt?" asked Beatrice.

"Call him," said Miss Sissy.

Beatrice sighed. She figured she better get used to this. Wyatt being Wyatt, had kindly set up a great rapport with the old woman. She quickly put together a plate of food and set it down in front of Miss Sissy before picking up the phone.

Beatrice walked into the kitchen again. "Wyatt? Do you have some time for a favor?"

"Of course I do," said Wyatt. "Is anything wrong?"

"Something *seems* to be wrong, but I'm not finding out what. Miss Sissy is here," said Beatrice.

Wyatt's voice was concerned, "Is she all right?"

"Definitely not. She's very agitated."

Wyatt gave a small chuckle. "Well, that's pretty standard, isn't it? Miss Sissy is always out of sorts."

Beatrice peered around the kitchen wall. "Yes. But I found her in my azalea bushes out back. And I gave her a huge plate of food and she hasn't even touched it. Not even the bacon."

"Coming right over," said Wyatt quickly before hanging up.

A few minutes later, Wyatt joined them. Beatrice made him a plate of food, too, since she'd made far too much breakfast, thinking that Miss Sissy would be behaving normally and eat several, heaping helpings.

When Miss Sissy saw Wyatt, she burst into tears again. Wyatt gathered her into his arms for a hug before sitting back to study her, holding her hands. "Now, Miss Sissy, please tell us what's happened so that Beatrice and I can start helping you."

The old woman took a deep breath. "Maisie," she said. "She's gone!"

Ordinarily, news of a missing cat in this situation would make Beatrice relax a little. After all, no one was seriously ill, there was no terrible medical diagnosis to face. Only a missing housecat. But Beatrice knew that Maisie was family to Miss Sissy. Maisie, a laid-back white cat, was a shared responsibility between Miss Sissy and Posy, who let her stay in the shop during the day. And Miss Sissy didn't really need anything to make her even more unstable.

Wyatt's face reflected Beatrice's concern. "Maisie is missing? For how long?"

Miss Sissy looked thoughtful. The details associated with the passing of time weren't exactly her forte.

Beatrice asked, "Was she gone last night? Or did you notice she was gone this morning?"

"Yesterday. Late afternoon," said the old woman, looking anxious.

Wyatt asked, "Was she at your house, then? Not at the store?"

Miss Sissy gave him a scornful look. "Maisie would *never* run from Posy's shop!"

"Of course not," said Wyatt quickly. "She was at your house and she slipped out the door?"

"Why didn't you come over to ask for help then?" asked Beatrice, feeling a bit exasperated. Finding the cat was going to be more difficult as time went on. And she was starting to feel as if her life was getting taken over by problem animals: first the neighbor's barking dog, and now the missing Maisie.

"I did come over!" snapped Miss Sissy, glaring at her in accusation. "You were gone!"

So it must have been when she'd taken Noo-noo for a walk or when she and Wyatt had already left for the dinner party.

"Savannah helped look," said Miss Sissy. "Before she had to go."

Savannah was another friend and fellow quilter who was a huge animal-lover, herself. Beatrice didn't have any trouble believing that Savannah was scouring the area to find the missing cat.

Wyatt said gently, "We're going to help look, too. But first, why don't you have something to eat? You didn't look for her all night, did you?"

Miss Sissy pressed her lips together stubbornly, refusing to grace his question with an answer.

Beatrice sighed, visions of Miss Sissy crawling through hedges and woods all night dancing through her head.

Miss Sissy finally, reluctantly, consented to eat something and Beatrice and Wyatt managed to eat, too. They first canvassed the nearby woods and yards, before hopping in Wyatt's car to drive slowly around. Then they parked his car in a different spot to search there. They spent a couple of hours calling for Maisie. But Maisie seemed as though she didn't want to be found.

Beatrice glanced at her watch as they stood in the middle of the woods. She had things to do—Meadow was probably trying to reach her and Piper was likely trying to get in touch, too. Beatrice had forgotten to grab her phone before she left. And she was sure that Wyatt had things to do, too. He was just too kind to stop hunting for Maisie, knowing Miss Sissy would probably keep looking all day long.

"Okay, Miss Sissy," said Beatrice firmly, "We didn't *immediately* find Maisie. This doesn't mean that Maisie isn't going to be found."

"Maybe she's out hunting chipmunks," offered Wyatt.

Miss Sissy gave him a scornful look as if Maisie was way too intelligent to hunt small striped, rodents.

"She's probably just having an adventure. And you know cats can come back home even *weeks* later. Remember that old story, *The Incredible Journey*?" asked Beatrice.

This comparison didn't appear to ease Miss Sissy's mind.

"But Wyatt and I, unfortunately, have some things we need to do today. Here's what we're going to do. I'm going to go back home and make up flyers with Maisie's picture on them. Wyatt can put a couple up at the church." She glanced at Wyatt to make sure this secular flyer was all right to post on the church bulletin board and he nodded. "Then I'll put some all around downtown."

Miss Sissy looked down at the grass and leaves below her feet.

Wyatt reached out and held her hand. "It's Maisie, Miss Sissy. Everyone knows who she is. Think about that. She's famous in Dappled Hills."

This made Miss Sissy brighten a little. "What picture?" she said to Beatrice.

"You mean what picture of Maisie? I'm sure I have a few of them from the shop on my phone." Beatrice reached for her pocket and patted it. "I forgot. I left my phone at home. But I know I have some pictures of her."

This didn't seem to satisfy the old woman.

"And if I find out the pictures *aren't* any good, I'll call Posy. She can email some pictures to me from the shop," said Beatrice. "And I'm going to be out and about in town today and will be sure to mention Maisy to everyone I know."

Miss Sissy considered this and then slowly nodded.

"Okay," said Wyatt with relief in his voice. "This sounds like a good plan."

"Then let's get back in the car and head back," said Beatrice firmly.

Wyatt dropped off Miss Sissy and then pulled into Beatrice's driveway. He said, "Uh oh. Looks like the cavalry came."

It certainly had. A very agitated Meadow stood at Beatrice's door, pounding and calling. Noo-noo was in the front window, talking back to Meadow with short, happy barks. Meadow swung around at the sound of the car engine and put her hands on her hips. Her long hair was slung loosely into a ponytail and she wore a mismatched top and skirt as if she'd just pulled something on to run over.

"She doesn't look happy," observed Wyatt wryly.

Beatrice sighed. "I didn't have my phone on me and she's probably been trying to call or text for two hours. I did tell her she could let me know what she found out from Ramsay."

A second later, Piper's car pulled quickly into Beatrice's driveway, behind Beatrice's.

"For heaven's sake," muttered Beatrice. "Meadow must have called Piper and gotten *her* all worked up, too. Can't a body leave the house for a little while without a phone these days?"

"If they'd been really worried, I'm sure they'd have given me a call. But good luck," said Wyatt with a smile as Beatrice climbed reluctantly out of the car.

Meadow said indignantly as Beatrice approached her, "I was worried about you! You didn't answer my calls. I thought that maybe you'd fallen and broken a hip or something. I even called Piper!"

"So I see," said Beatrice with a sigh, pulling out her key to unlock her front door. "I'm hoping I'm years away from that possibility. Here, why don't you go on inside and I'll be there in a minute. Piper is probably on her way over to the school to help set up her classroom for the next year. Let me talk to her for a second."

Piper was indeed on her way to the school, but hopped out of the car to give her mother a hug. "Meadow told me what happened last night. How awful!"

"It was, for sure. Poor Caspian. It was quite a shock, having something like that happen at a dinner party," said Beatrice. And it was. She thought again about the moment she'd found out that he was dead—and shivered. "But we were fine ... no worries, Piper."

"Are you sure? I can go in later to work, if you'd like to talk it over. You've got so much going on right now, trying to get ready for the wedding that I hate that you had any more stress," said Piper, looking concerned.

"Oh, I think Meadow plans to talk it over, never you fear," said Beatrice dryly. "And you've got your own wedding to stew over. Don't worry about me—I'm just fine."

"All right then." Piper gave Beatrice another quick hug. "I'll check in with you later, okay?" And she drove away.

Meadow, who had helped herself to a cup of likely stale coffee, was still fussing when Beatrice walked inside. "Honestly, Beatrice, anything could have happened to you. I'll admit that a health-related thing did pop into my mind first, but it could have been anything. Maybe you'd had a visit from our local killer. Since there *is* one on the loose," said Meadow.

Beatrice looked quickly over at Meadow. "There is? Ramsay confirmed it?"

Beatrice stooped to rub Noo-noo. She rolled over and grinned at Beatrice as she rubbed her tummy.

Meadow plopped down on the sofa, holding her coffee cup, and said, "He sure did. Ramsay said that Caspian was drugged and then smothered. The poor man."

Beatrice sat down in an overstuffed armchair. "Drugged *and* smothered. I guess someone wanted to make sure he didn't struggle or fight back. He was a big man, despite his age. I don't think I realized how big he *was* until I really saw him up close. It would have been easy enough to drug him since he wasn't exactly fixing his own drinks. And he did set his drink down some, too, which would give plenty of opportunity to doctor it."

Meadow waved her hands around animatedly. "What I can't believe is that someone would do something like that at a *party*. With all of us there! With the chief of *police* there, for heaven's sake!"

Beatrice said in a thoughtful voice, "It would have to be someone pretty brazen. Or maybe not. After all, it wasn't as if we were *looking* for someone to be murdered. We weren't trying to observe and take note of every little thing. It was a *party*."

"Not much of one," muttered Meadow.

"At any rate, no one was expecting a murder to take place," said Beatrice. She frowned. "I'm trying to remember how Caspian appeared when he said he was going to lie down before dinner. Did he seem drugged then?"

"He seemed curt and dismissive like he did the rest of the evening," said Meadow tartly.

"And still alert," said Beatrice. "Maybe it was still taking effect. What kind of drug was it ... did Ramsay say?"

"Run of the mill sleeping pills, apparently. Caspian had an automatically filled prescription and apparently rarely used the pills." Meadow sighed. "Someone must have taken a bunch of them and crushed them up."

Beatrice said with a frown, "Wouldn't that have been awfully bitter? I wouldn't think he'd have drunk anything that tasted bad."

"Caspian was drinking Manhattans, and they must have masked the taste," said Meadow with a shrug. "They have Angostura bitters in them."

Beatrice said, "Although, now that I think about it, I don't think he drank very much of his last drink. Maybe it didn't taste as good as the others."

"I'm not sure. But I'm starting to feel sorry for the old coot. He wasn't the friendliest guy, but he didn't deserve to be killed by his own family that way!" said Meadow.

"We're sure it *was* his family, right?" asked Beatrice. "What did Ramsay say about that?"

"Well, it wasn't a robbery. Unless someone had a grudge against Caspian, I can't imagine why a non-family member would murder Caspian." Meadow stopped. "You don't suppose someone like Wynona could have done something like this, do you?"

Noo-noo looked up at Beatrice and she gently lifted the corgi into her lap. Absently petting her, she said, "Wynona? I thought you were saying that she had a grudge against Hawkins, not Caspian."

"But Caspian was the source of all the trouble. He was the one who forbade Hawkins to marry Wynona," said Meadow.

"You're still making the whole thing sound like a performance of *Romeo and Juliet*," said Beatrice.

"It *was* sort of like that," said Meadow. She made a face. "But I don't like thinking of Wynona being responsible. Besides, how would she have gotten in?"

Beatrice said wryly, "That house was hardly a fortress. I saw Barkis, the groundskeeper, inside while we were having our tour. I think anyone could have slipped in and no one would notice. The front door wasn't even locked as guests were arriving."

"You don't think *Barkis* would have done it?" asked Meadow.

Beatrice shook her head. "Why on earth would he want to? He'd have nothing to gain and everything to lose. What happens if Hawkins or Malcolm decides to fire him? No, he had more job security with Caspian around."

Meadow nodded, taking it all in. Then she said, "All right, tell me what was going on this morning that you were gone so early. And why you didn't answer your phone!"

Beatrice said, "I was awakened this morning by Noo-noo growling at me. I expected to see some sort of prowler and instead I saw Miss Sissy hanging out in my azalea bushes."

"What on earth was she doing in there?"

Beatrice said, "Looking for Maisie."

Meadow gasped and put her hands in front of her mouth. "Oh no. Maisie is missing? Was Miss Sissy totally devastated over it?"

"She was very upset, yes. She even cried, which really startled me. But Meadow, I'm sure Maisie will be fine. We'll put up some flyers and tell some folks about it and before you know it, half of Dappled Hills will be out looking for the cat," said Beatrice.

Meadow brightened. "That's exactly what we need to do. We'll make some flyers and put them out. Besides, that will also give us a chance to snoop around a little. We've got to give Ramsay a helping hand, you know. I think he relies on us now."

Beatrice laughed. "I don't know about that. But I did want to poke around and see what we can find out. What happened last night has really sort of made me mad. It was supposed to be a night of celebration and instead there was a tragedy. I want to get to the bottom of it all. Besides, Wyatt was actually fond of Caspian."

"That's because he likes everybody, even crusty old men. But I'm with you on this—there's something very sad about the whole thing. And we have a murderer in Dappled Hills! That cannot be allowed. All right, first things first. Where are your pictures of Maisie the cat?" demanded Meadow.

Beatrice glanced around her. "Good question. They're on my phone, which I still haven't found." She thought for a moment. "But since I was awakened by a growling Noo-noo, I'm going to guess that it's still in my bedroom. I didn't exactly have a normal start to my day."

Beatrice found the phone on her bedside table, still on the charger, and thumbed through the pictures in her gallery. She dubiously handed the phone over to Meadow, who squinted at it.

"This is Maisie? This is a horrible picture of Maisie. What else have you got on here?" asked Meadow.

Apparently, at least according to Meadow, there were no good pictures of the cat to be found on Beatrice's device.

Meadow said, "Let's go to the Patchwork Cottage. Posy is bound to have some cute pictures of Maisie that will actually make people *want* to find her. And besides, I have an errand to run over there. But first we should head over to the Nelms home. After all, they suffered a terrible tragedy last night. We should bring food."

Beatrice said wryly, "And I'm guessing that you've already made plans to prepare something."

"I had a hard time sleeping after Ramsay came in, so I headed for the kitchen. Fried chicken, cornbread, mashed potatoes, and coleslaw!" Meadow said.

Beatrice felt her mouth water and realized that she must have burned off the bits of breakfast that she'd had with Miss Sissy. "Sounds great."

"I think it's the perfect meal for the grieving family," said Meadow. "And it smells so good that they should let us right in the door." She studied Beatrice. "You look hungry. Have you eaten today or did the Miss Sissy mess take over your mealtime?"

"I did eat a little, but I either didn't eat enough, or I burned it all off by searching through the woods looking for Maisie," admitted Beatrice.

"Then let's plan on eating lunch downtown after we go by the Nelms house and the Patchwork Cottage. I think the only way I'll be able to see you at all with all the wedding festivities is if I steal you away for lunch," said Meadow.

Beatrice fed Noo-noo and let her out, and then she and Meadow got into Meadow's van. They stopped by Meadow's house to pick up the food, which immediately made Beatrice's stomach growl. Meadow could be annoying sometimes, but she was a fantastic cook.

Chapter Five

Meadow pulled into the circular driveway outside the Nelms estate. Because now, in broad daylight, the size of the property around the mansion was clear.

Meadow said, "You know, if I were a missing cat, this is where I'd want to go. Look at this place! There's a barn and all these outbuildings and things. There are probably all kinds of things for a cat to hunt around here."

They scanned as far as they could see, but only saw the grouchy-looking groundskeeper glaring at them from across a field.

"Barkis looks more sour than he usually does," said Meadow.

"He looks like he blames us for all the ruckus last night," said Beatrice.

Meadow said indignantly, "We were just the poor, unsuspecting guests!"

"Maybe we can speak to him on the way out," said Beatrice in a thoughtful voice. "He might have seen something last night."

"From way out in the barn?" asked Meadow as they got out of the car.

Beatrice said, "I saw him go in and out of the house. I've no idea what he was doing."

"Then we should ask!" said Meadow. "I know what you said about his having no motive, but still. I wonder if Ramsay and the state police have questioned him. They might not have realized that he was in the house around the time of the murder."

They walked up the walkway and knocked on the front door. Then they knocked again.

Meadow frowned. "It's definitely not too early to come by. You don't suppose there's been more foul play?"

But right then the door opened. Hawkins stood there, looking at them blankly, as if he'd never seen them before. He was wearing pajama pants and a ratty-looking tee shirt. His hair was mussed up as though he hadn't combed it out after he woke up this morning. Hawkins looked like someone who was coming undone.

Meadow said brightly, "Hawkins! We're so sorry about your father. I could hardly sleep last night, worrying over it. I've made some fried chicken and sides for you and the family. Are they here?"

Hawkins took the food from her robotically. He hesitated over her question. "I don't know. I don't think so. It's been quiet inside."

"Well then, they can have some when they come back home," said Meadow.

Beatrice said, "Thanks again for hosting last night. Wyatt and I are so sorry that the evening turned out the way it did."

Hawkins nodded, looking at the floor as he did.

It was becoming obvious that it wasn't going to occur to Hawkins to invite them inside. Since there was apparently no one else around to be a good host, Beatrice decided to prompt him.

"I'm sorry to be a bother, especially with everything you must be dealing with, but may I have a glass of water?" asked Beatrice.

Hawkins automatically started going through the motions of hosting: inviting them in, gesturing to chairs in the drawing room, and then going off in search of water.

Meadow heaved a sigh and said in her stage whisper volume to Beatrice, "Wow, he's being weird."

"I guess everyone grieves in a different way," said Beatrice with a shrug. But as she said it, she realized that she wasn't really getting a grieving vibe from Hawkins. Instead, he seemed more anxious and spacy than anything else.

He returned a minute later with a large glass tumbler full of water and one ice cube. He thrust it at Meadow.

Meadow reached over and handed it to Beatrice, rolling her eyes in the process.

Beatrice took a large sip and then cleared her throat. "Thank you, Hawkins. I'm sorry to impose on you like this. Meadow and I just wanted to express our condolences in person."

Meadow nodded vigorously.

Hawkins said woodenly, "Thank you."

Beatrice waited for him to continue, but when it became obvious that nothing else was to be forthcoming, she said, "I was trying to reconstruct the events of the evening to see if I could help offer any information to the police. But I'm afraid that I must not have seen anything very helpful."

"Neither did I," Meadow asserted quickly.

"Did you happen to see anything that would help us know who was behind your father's death?" asked Beatrice.

Hawkins's blank face grew more animated. He said, "Sadie. It's got to be Sadie, doesn't it? Yes, that's what makes sense."

He seemed almost to be talking to himself, not Beatrice and Meadow. Beatrice said slowly, "Why do you think your sister might be responsible?"

Hawkins turned his blue eyes on her. "Isn't it obvious? She couldn't stand him. Sadie even left town for years so that she wouldn't have to interact with Father. They were estranged."

Meadow tried to be delicate. "I remember, Hawkins. I just don't remember why they were estranged to begin with."

Hawkins didn't seem to be in the mood to pick up on Meadow's subtlety. He brooded, "Sadie always thought she was better than all of us. Looks down on us all the time like a goody-goody."

"What kind of work does she do?" asked Beatrice.

"She's a social worker for the county. Sadie acts like she's Mother Theresa or something and that the rest of the family is oh so wicked because we have just the slightest interest in money. Acting like she wouldn't like money, herself!" said Hawkins.

Beatrice said, "But you didn't actually see anything or hear anything that could be proof that Sadie was involved last night?"

Hawkins thought for a minute as if he was trying to conjure up something, and then reluctantly shook his head.

Meadow said, "What were *you* doing when your father died? You'd left the tour and all."

Beatrice shifted uncomfortably and took another sip of her water. Trust Meadow to be direct.

Hawkins frowned. "I just wanted to top off my drink, that's all. And check on the caterers. I knew I wasn't going to miss anything, after all—I know this house like the back of my hand. And why would I want to kill my father? I don't need any money. Besides, Barkis saw me when I left the tour, while he was inside getting something."

Beatrice said, "Did you and your father get along?"

Hawkins said, "Well enough. Father didn't really get along with anyone."

Beatrice stood up. "Well, we should be going. Again, we're so sorry about Caspian."

Meadow stood up, too. "We are." She looked across the room at a table near the front door. "And ... um, you may want to go ahead and just stick that chicken and sides in the fridge real quick."

Hawkins nodded, but his mind was clearly somewhere else.

"Ten dollars says that Hawkins is going to leave that food out and that it will be inedible by the time Sadie and Malcolm get back home," fumed Meadow as they walked away from the house.

"He was definitely out to lunch. Stress, I guess," said Beatrice. She stopped walking and scanned the field in front of her. "Where is that Barkis? I think we should have a word with him."

"I think that's him over there," said Meadow.

They walked over to the old man who was picking up limbs from the bushes he was trimming. Barkis had a wad of chewing tobacco in his cheek, a dismissive expression, and wore old khaki pants and an equally-ancient button-down blue shirt. He continued working as they approached.

"Hi Barkis," said Meadow. "It's been a while since I've seen you."

Barkis's response to this was to spit some of the tobacco. Fortunately, this was in the opposite direction of Beatrice and Meadow.

Since Barkis was apparently not a fan of social niceties, Beatrice decided to launch right into the subject of the murder.

"Shocking what happened last night," said Beatrice.

Barkis raised his gaze to meet hers and gave a curt nod.

Meadow said, "You've worked for Caspian a long time, haven't you?"

He gave her a scornful look. "You should know, living here your whole life. I started out in the grounds here when he was just a teenager. Worked for his folks."

"And you liked him?" asked Beatrice.

Barkis shrugged a shoulder. "Weren't my job to like him or not. My job was to take care of things." He crushed the limbs into a wheelbarrow to make them fit better.

"Would you say that his family liked him?" asked Beatrice.

He narrowed his eyes at her. "You're asking because he was murdered? Could've been anyone."

Beatrice said, "Maybe it could. But it's most likely a member of his own family. What do you think of them?"

He scowled. "Vultures. Hanging around, waiting for Caspian to die. Useless, all of them."

Meadow said, "And they didn't get along with Caspian well, did they?"

Barkis spat again. "They argued with him. Stressed him out. Worthless."

"You've known them all their lives, haven't you? What are your impressions of them?" asked Beatrice.

Barkis heaved a long-suffering sigh as if he knew he wouldn't be able to get on with his work until he'd answered the questions to their satisfaction.

"That Hawkins? He's nothing like his father. Doesn't have the brains or the guts. Caspian was always ashamed of him. He just wants to sponge off his father. Got no money of his own and Caspian was cutting him off," said Barkis.

Beatrice decided that Caspian definitely wouldn't be a candidate for Father of the Year. He apparently hadn't gotten the memo that children aren't going to be carbon copies of their parents.

Meadow said, "Hawkins said he saw you before Caspian died. And that you saw him."

Barkis lifted a dirt-encrusted eyebrow.

Beatrice added, "He was acting as if you were his alibi. That he couldn't have been with his father because you saw him."

"Is that so?" asked Barkis coolly. "Well, I don't rightly know about that."

Meadow said, "It was kind of silly anyway, since he wasn't saying he was with you the *entire* hour that poor Caspian could have been attacked in."

"What do you make of the rest of the family?" asked Beatrice. "Since you didn't think that Hawkins was as sharp as his father."

"That Sadie? She's right smart. When she was a little girl, she was the one who'd come up with all sorts of games for them to play. They always played together—hardly ever had any outside friends to come by. She was smart like Caspian. But he thought she'd wasted her brains through her job. Caspian thought she could be a high-level banker or do investments or something like that. But she ended up with the poor." Barkis's face reflected his astonishment at Sadie's career path.

So Caspian was a controlling father, as well, trying to steer his children. He must have been furious when they defied him.

"What about Malcolm?" asked Beatrice. "What do you think of Caspian's younger son?"

Barkis spat at the ground in a gesture that seemed to sum up his opinion quite well. "Slick," he offered. He started moving away from them, toward another wheelbarrow that had paving bricks in it.

Meadow called after him. "Wait!"

Barkis turned around with a contemptuous look. "What now?" he growled.

"Have you seen this cat?" asked Meadow. "Go on, Beatrice, pull up that picture on your phone."

Beatrice fumbled the phone as she pulled it out of the pocket of her khaki slacks. She found a picture and handed it to Barkis.

Barkis frowned, considering the picture. "That's a cat?" he asked.

"The picture isn't *that* bad," said Beatrice, irritated.

"It ain't that *good*, neither," grunted Barkis. "Can't say that I've seen it. Seen a wild old woman, though. Sticks in her hair."

It sounded as though Miss Sissy was starting to really canvas the area.

A few minutes later, Beatrice and Meadow were back in the car.

"I think he's on something," said Meadow huffily.

"Barkis? Well, he's definitely on chewing tobacco," said Beatrice making a face. "I guess he doesn't spend enough time around people to perfect his social graces."

"No, no, I didn't mean Barkis. I meant *Hawkins*. He's got to be on something, doesn't he? With that vacant stare? What was going on with him?" asked Meadow.

"To be charitable, I guess that could be his method of grieving. But I don't really think he was grieving. And I don't think, as you say, that he is 'on something.' I think he's worried," said Beatrice slowly.

"Yes, you were saying something like that earlier," said Meadow with a frown. "What do you mean, though? What on earth is he worried about?"

"I wondered if his behavior isn't some sort of manifestation of his guilt. Maybe he's worried that he's going to be found out and that he'll be arrested and jailed for killing his father," suggested Beatrice.

"Well then, he should stop acting so weird then!" said Meadow. "He could start by being a bit more effusive over my fried chicken. I spent a good deal of time over that!"

"I'm sure they'll all love it," said Beatrice.

"Assuming he even puts it in the refrigerator," muttered Meadow.

"Moving on to other subjects, we're still heading to the Patchwork Cottage, aren't we?" asked Beatrice.

"Of course. We clearly can't make flyers using your pictures of Maisie. They'll frighten people off instead of making them want to find her!"

When they walked into the Patchwork Cottage a few minutes later, Beatrice felt again that sense of relaxation and peace that came over her when she was there. The quilt shop was cheerful and cozy with soft bluegrass music playing, cheery gingham curtains hanging in the windows, and quilts hanging everywhere. There was lots of sunlight pouring into the shop and the shop's owner, Posy, greeted them with a smile. She was a small, older woman with kind eyes and a fondness for fluffy cardigans.

Beatrice sadly noted that a sunbeam that should have had a sleeping Maisie in it was vacant. What's more, she had the clear realization that the happy, relaxed Posy didn't know anything about the fact that Maisie was missing. Miss Sissy must not have wanted to worry her with it—or to admit that the cat had slipped out on her watch.

Meadow apparently made the same realization at the same time. She gave Beatrice a panicked look and muttered an excuse about powdering her nose. She obviously didn't want to be the bearer of bad news.

Chapter Six

Beatrice decided to cut to the chase since time was of the essence when finding a lost cat. "Posy, I hate to have to tell you this, but Maisie is missing. Miss Sissy came by my house this morning, looking for her. She hasn't shown up here, has she?" she finished, hopefully.

Posy's normally sunny expression clouded up. "No, she sure hasn't. I hope we can find poor Maisie—she must be so scared. She never goes outside! How is Miss Sissy handling things?"

"About as you'd expect. She was pretty wild when I saw her. Wyatt and I searched for a couple of hours this morning and I think Miss Sissy has been searching for her much longer than that—I'm wondering if she even went to bed last night. I'm sure we'll find Maisie, though," said Beatrice.

Posy said, "I should help Miss Sissy search. Let me call my part-time helper and see if she can cover the store for me while I'm gone."

"I think the more eyes that are looking for Maisie the better, but I think we also need to spread the word, first. I don't have any good pictures of the cat—have you got better ones? We can make posters and flyers really quickly and hang them around town. Someone is bound to find her then," said Beatrice.

Posy hurried off to make the phone call to her employee and to search her phone for pictures. Meadow came back out from the back of the store, looking sheepish.

"Sorry," she muttered to Beatrice. "Posy is so sweet and I couldn't bear to break the news to her. How is she taking it?"

"The cat's not *dead*, Meadow, only missing. She seemed mostly concerned about Miss Sissy," said Beatrice.

"Isn't that just like Posy?" said Meadow. "Always so sweet."

Posy joined them and said, "It's all set. I've got Amy coming over now to cover me and I'm making flyers in the meantime. Then I'll join Miss Sissy in searching."

"We will, too," said Meadow quickly.

But Posy was shaking her head. "I appreciate it, Meadow, but I have the feeling that maybe this will give me the opportunity to calm Miss Sissy down. It sounds like she's pretty keyed up right now. Maybe you could all help by distributing the flyers and posters?" she asked.

Fifteen minutes later, Amy was at the cash register and Posy was leaving to look for Miss Sissy. Beatrice and Meadow both held tape and a stack of posters with a much more accurate depiction of the missing Maisie.

They walked out the front door onto the sidewalk and then Meadow stopped short. "Look, Beatrice!" she hissed. "It's Malcolm! In the ice cream shop."

Beatrice said, "Let's go express our sympathy. And tell him that there's a fried chicken dinner that may or may not be in his fridge."

The ice cream shop was fairly quiet. Malcolm appeared to have a large bowl of multi-colored scoops of ice cream. His handsome face was somber and he didn't look as though the ice cream was really cheering him up.

Malcolm gave a small smile and stood up when he saw them approach. "Sorry that last night's festivities didn't go according to plan," he said.

Meadow gave him a fierce and rather unexpected hug, startling Malcolm a little. "Don't you worry about that! We felt terrible about how things ended up. How are you? How is the family?"

Beatrice cleared her throat. "We did stop by the house to bring some food by—Meadow's cooking, not mine. Hawkins was there."

Malcolm made a face. "Then you saw how he was. Father's death seems to have hit him really hard, somehow. The rest of us are all right—at least we're coping. We've been trying to figure out the details for the service and all. I'm here waiting for Della ... she's at the Patchwork Cottage now. We needed a break from planning funerals and talking to police."

Beatrice frowned. "We must have just missed her, then. Or maybe we couldn't see her around some of Posy's displays. We were just in there. Posy's and Miss Sissy's cat Maisie is missing. She's the shop cat for the Patchwork Cottage." She gestured to the flyers she held.

Malcolm nodded and held his hand out for a flyer. He studied the photo and then handed it back to Beatrice. "I'll keep an eye out. I know how attached people are to their pets. And vice-versa. Maybe we wouldn't even be in the situation we're in right now if Father had owned a large dog that never left his side."

Beatrice said, "What do you think happened last night?"

Malcolm sighed and said in a very matter-of-fact voice, "Well, Ramsay left absolutely no doubt that it was murder. And he didn't think much of a theory that it might be someone other than the family. Ramsay said that a murderer would have to have a screw loose to enter a house while a party was going on and then randomly kill the patriarch. Besides, we're the only ones who could have doctored Father's drink."

"What a terrible thing to have to suspect your own sister and brother of murder!" said Meadow, putting a hand to her chest.

"I agree. It's certainly not helping us all pull together after Father's death. I hate to think that any of us could be responsible for something like that. But ... I think that my brother has got to be the one responsible. I know *I* didn't do it. And I don't think Sadie did, either. Hawkins's behavior has been so erratic lately. Frankly, he's a disaster."

"In what way?" asked Beatrice.

"He was on the edge even before Father's death and now it looks like he's heading over the edge completely. Something is worrying Hawkins and he drinks too much to try and forget whatever it is that's worrying him. I overheard him arguing with Father only a week ago," said Malcolm.

"What were they arguing about?" asked Meadow rather breathlessly.

"Money. Hawkins wanted money and Father didn't want him to have any—said he'd waste it, as usual. Hawkins tried demanding it and pleading for it and Father wouldn't budge. I know that Hawkins was gambling months ago and I know that Hawkins doesn't have the best of luck. I can only assume that he built up some substantial gambling debts."

"Is he still gambling?" asked Beatrice.

Malcolm swallowed a bite of his ice cream, then gave a flat laugh. "He can't gamble without any money. No, he's broken that habit. Hawkins sort of fell apart when his relationship with Wynona ended. That's when he started a lot of self-destructive behavior."

Beatrice waited for Malcolm to elaborate. When he didn't show any signs of continuing, Beatrice asked, "It definitely seemed to me that there was some tension between both Hawkins and Sadie and your father. Did you get along well with him, yourself?"

Malcolm smiled, showing his perfect teeth in his tanned face. "We got along amicably enough. Oh, I'm not saying there weren't times when he really got on my nerves. And we've had the occasional argument. But it's not as if we were at each other's throats all the time or anything. He and I had similar interests at least, unlike Father and Hawkins or Sadie."

"Sadie didn't get along with her Father?" asked Beatrice.

Malcolm chuckled, "Well, you know that they were estranged for years, don't you? For the most part, over her life, she and Father haven't seen eye to eye. But she's certainly been trying to make up with him over the past year. Sadie has made herself very helpful to Father and has tried to warm up to him."

"Did it work?" asked Meadow. "Had they been friendlier with each other?"

Malcolm shrugged. "Hard to say. Father wasn't one for really showing his feelings. I think there was still a lot of tension between them. Sadie has this really condescending attitude a lot of the time. She seems to think she's better than the rest of the family since she works with the poor."

"Does that bother you?" asked Beatrice.

Malcolm shrugged again, "Not really. I respect her for going her own way. You wouldn't believe it by looking at her now, but growing up she was completely different. She looked like a hippie—long hair, long flowing clothes, flowers in her hair."

"Maybe she just took it to another level. She decided that the best way to use her hippie values was to work with the needy," said Beatrice.

Malcolm shrugged. "You're probably right."

"Well, it was good talking to you. Again, we're so sorry about what happened. Let me know if I can run errands for you or help with Caspian's service in any way. We'll go and let you finish your ice cream," said Beatrice.

Meadow gave Beatrice a wink when Malcolm wasn't looking. "I forgot to get one thing at the Patchwork Cottage, Beatrice. Can we run back there for a few minutes?"

"Sure," said Beatrice. Clearly Meadow thought this was a good opportunity to catch Della without Malcolm being around. Della was sure to be more forthcoming about the family and what she thought about them without her boyfriend being right there.

"Maybe you can check on Della for me," said Malcolm lightly. "Make sure she's not buying up half the Patchwork Cottage."

As Beatrice and Meadow headed for the door, he added, "Thanks for dropping the food by."

Meadow said, "Just a heads-up that the fried chicken dinner may or may not be in the fridge. We asked Hawkins to put it in there, but he was a little—well ..."

"Out to lunch?" asked Malcolm. "Thanks for letting me know. I'll follow up on it when we get back."

Meadow said, "Let's go find Della while we've got the chance."

"He didn't look like he was anywhere close to finishing that huge bowl of ice cream, so I think we have a few minutes," said Beatrice.

Posy's part-time helper was busily trying to check-out customers and answer the phone at the same time as they walked back in.

Beatrice glanced around the room and said, "There she is."

Della, dressed somewhat somberly in a black top and gray slacks, was holding a basket full of notions and was carefully studying others.

Beatrice and Meadow walked over to her and she started a little as if she'd been in her own world. Then she gave them a polite smile. "Oh, hello."

Meadow said in her most sincere voice, "Beatrice and I just wanted to say how very sorry we were about Caspian's death."

"It must have been such a horrible shock to you last night," added Beatrice.

Della nodded and set her heavy basket down on the floor. "It sure was. I couldn't sleep a wink last night, I was so wound up."

Della, with her glossy hair and bright eyes didn't look like someone who hadn't had enough sleep. But Beatrice decided she was being uncharitable. Maybe Della was able to cover up exhaustion better than most.

"We saw Malcolm next door a few minutes ago, and he mentioned you were in here," said Beatrice.

Della said, "Well, we've been doing so much this morning that we thought we should take a break. Planning the service, writing the obituary, and what-not. You can't do it all day long without going a little kooky. I thought I'd stop by the Patchwork Cottage to relax a little bit. I'm still trying to figure out what I'm doing with quilting and Posy is always *so* helpful. But I guess she's not here today."

"Actually, she was here, but left to search for her cat," said Beatrice.

Della's eyes grew wide. "You mean that sweetheart of a cat that hangs out here? Maisie? Oh, the poor thing."

Meadow nodded solemnly. "Maisie was with Miss Sissy and escaped. Posy is trying to help her search."

"Seems like there's a lot going on," said Della shaking her head.

Beatrice said, "Do you have any idea who might have been responsible for what happened to Caspian last night? Or did you see or hear anything? I feel terrible that it happened during an event for Wyatt and me."

Della made a face. "People are wicked. And yes, I know exactly who's responsible. I told the police about it. Your Ramsay is so nice, Meadow."

Meadow smiled at her.

Beatrice said quickly, "Wait. You *know* who the murderer is? Who is it?"

"Wynona Thigpen, of course," said Della, spitting out the name as if it tasted bad.

"Wynona?" gasped Meadow and Beatrice in unison.

Beatrice said, "How do you know? She wasn't at the party. Did she slip in?"

Della rolled her eyes. "I didn't see her, but she wouldn't have *wanted* to be seen, would she? She'd have been sneaking around. I've caught her there in the house before, wanting to talk to Hawkins. Can you believe it? You'd think if someone dumped you, your pride would be so hurt that you wouldn't want to show up uninvited and beg him to take you back."

"Is that what happened?" asked Meadow, gaping.

"It did one time. And another time she showed up just to tell Hawkins off," said Della. She was clearly not impressed with either of these tactics.

"What did Hawkins do when she showed up?" asked Beatrice.

"Oh, he couldn't get rid of her fast enough! The last thing that Hawkins wanted was to upset his father anymore about this. After all, Caspian was the one who basically decreed that Hawkins dump

Wynona. That's why Wynona hated Caspian—and ended up hating Hawkins, too. She seems like she'll *never* get over it and now she's a spinster!" Della spat out the last.

Beatrice didn't think that people really used the word *spinster* any longer. She said, "That's very interesting. Wynona is actually in charge of helping with the flowers for my wedding."

This bit of information didn't seem to faze Della at all. She rolled her eyes. "Can you imagine having to help with weddings every week when you know you'll never be married yourself?"

Meadow frowned. "Wynona wasn't exactly left at the altar, Della. They weren't even engaged, as I recall."

"They were practically as good as engaged," said Della, looking just the slightest bit sulky. "Wynona sure thought they were. I think she was even looking at dresses and everything!" She made a quick pivot in subject and said to Beatrice, "What kind of dress are you getting? I know you told me last night about some of your colors and the reception and all, but you didn't say anything about the dress. I bet it's beautiful!"

Beatrice said, "Since it's a second wedding for both of us, I chose to get a gray, lace dress."

Now it was Meadow's turn to roll her eyes. "Like that gives anyone a mental image of the dress. It's lovely, Della. It's a sleeveless, knee-length gray sheath with a beautiful gray lace overlay. It has a sheer front and back yoke, a round neckline, and a scalloped hem."

Della grinned at Meadow. "Thank you! I can actually picture it now."

"You're very welcome," said Meadow with a chuckle. "I don't think describing clothing is something that Beatrice does particularly well. Although she has many other gifts!"

Beatrice smiled at them. "I never could have conjured up the dress the way you did, Meadow."

Della's face grew dreamy. "I've known exactly what my wedding dress will look like since I started dating Malcolm."

Beatrice and Meadow exchanged glances. Beatrice said, "I'm so sorry—I didn't realize that you'd set a date."

Della shot Beatrice an annoyed look. "The date hasn't been set yet, but we *are* engaged. Malcolm and I simply kept it under the radar so that Caspian wouldn't act out. I didn't think he *would* act out, but considering he liked pushing people around, we didn't want to give him the chance. I'm going to be wearing this gorgeous designer dress. It's the prettiest thing I've ever seen."

Beatrice decided to redirect the conversation before she ended up with another example of how to describe a dress. "It sounds lovely, Della. You know, Meadow and I were talking before we came in the shop and saying what a shame it was that neither she nor I really heard or saw anything that could help the police to find Caspian's murderer."

Della shrugged. "I didn't either. I was getting ready for the dinner, then I was on the tour, and then I was visiting with everybody in the drawing room as they came in. I was totally shocked."

Beatrice said, "Oh, I thought you'd left the drawing room once or twice, that maybe you'd have seen something."

Della lifted an eyebrow. "Only to use the powder room before dinner. That's all." She picked up her shopping basket again as if to signal that their conversation was coming to a close. "If you're looking for who's responsible, I've already told you that it's Wynona. Go talk with her."

Beatrice said quickly before they lost Della completely, "Do you think now that Caspian has passed away, that Hawkins and Wynona will end up together again?"

Della looked surprised, as if this possibility hadn't occurred to her. Then she said slowly, "You know, I suppose they could. Although Hawkins has been upset about Wynona's appearances at the house and the way she's talked about him in town. Still, I think he might have feelings for her."

Meadow said, "What makes you say that?"

"Because he still has pictures of her in his room. And I don't think they're to remind him of the mistake he made in dating her," said Della with a smug look. She looked at her watch. "I've got to finish up my shopping now. Good seeing you two."

But her smile didn't reach her eyes.

Chapter Seven

"Well, Della sure threw Wynona under the bus," said Meadow, shaking her head as she and Beatrice ate lunch together.

Beatrice said, "But it makes sense that she would. After all, blaming Wynona diverts attention from the family. Della obviously plans on being a member of that family in the near future."

Meadow snorted. "So did Wynona. I wonder if Malcolm is really onboard with it all. And I wonder if Caspian was all that happy about Malcolm's relationship with Della. Did you know that Della would be Malcolm's *third* wife?"

"Maybe the third time is the charm?" asked Beatrice lightly. She had another bite of her chicken salad sandwich.

"It's hard to imagine that it would be. And not that I want to ever discourage anyone from taking up quilting, but I'd gotten the impression last week from Posy that Della might have started quilting to please Malcolm. His mother was apparently very crafty and he's always really admired women who are artistic. Maybe Della's trying to play that up. She's definitely determined to put a ring on his finger." Meadow emphatically waved her fork in the air.

"Speaking of putting rings on fingers, I've really got to get back home. I've got a meeting with Wynona and I think Wyatt was going to try and make it, too," said Beatrice. "You wouldn't think that a small wedding would take this much planning, but it almost seems as though it takes as much planning as a big wedding. At any rate, maybe I can ask Wynona a few questions while she's there to go over the food with us—just sort of slip the questions in."

Meadow said, "You shouldn't have a hard time asking her questions—she's always happy to talk about Hawkins. It's just not talking about him in a *good* way."

"Do you think that Della was right? That Hawkins actually still has feelings for her? And Wynona for him? Because, now that Caspian is out of the way, they could resume their relationship," said Beatrice.

"With all the harsh words between them, I wouldn't have said so, but you just never know. Love sometimes conquers all!" said Meadow.

Beatrice nodded. "I suppose so. There's just something about Della. She seems as though she simply wanted to stab Wynona in the back."

After they finished eating, Meadow dropped Beatrice off at the house. "Let me know how it goes with Wynona!" she said, tapping her horn cheerily as she left. This made Noo-noo's little face appear in the window. When she spotted Beatrice, she gave her a big, doggy grin.

Inside, Beatrice stooped to rub Noo-noo and give her a hug. "I've been gone a lot today, haven't I?" It was a good thing that Wynona was actually going to drop by and see *her* instead of the other way around.

Beatrice took Noo-noo for a short walk and then came in to take a nap, since she'd missed so much sleep lately with the barking of the neighbor's dog. When she woke up, she found it was time to make a quick bite of supper before Wynona and Wyatt came over to talk about the flowers. She'd picked up some beautiful heirloom tomatoes at a produce stand the day before and they'd ripened to perfection on her kitchen counter. She made a tomato sandwich with mayonnaise. Usually adding anything to a tomato sandwich was something Beatrice considered a sacrilege, but today she couldn't resist adding a slice of white American cheese. Paired with some red grapes, it made her the perfect light meal.

She'd just finished tidying up in the kitchen and living room when there was a light tap on her door. Noo-noo gave a happy yelp and Beatrice opened the door to a smiling Wyatt who stooped to pet the corgi. Wynona pulled into the driveway right behind Wyatt and waved at them.

Wynona always looked chic in her trademark black. Today, she was wearing black, tailored cropped pants and a black tunic paired with a necklace of different colored stones. Beatrice had gotten the impression from Wynona that money was always tight and never something to be relied on in the wedding business. To get more business, she expanded her reach to nearby towns and was frequently on the go. Although Beatrice and Wyatt were having a very small wedding, Beatrice wanted some small arrangements for the service, and she also considered Wynona a friend that she felt she should give a little business to. Even if it *was* very little business.

Wynona gave Beatrice a quick hug and beamed at Wyatt and her. "Getting excited?" she asked.

Beatrice said, "Yes," and smiled at Wyatt, who reached out to squeeze her hand. In that moment, she *was* excited. She didn't think about the events still to come, the things she needed to do, the phone calls she needed to make, or the preparations she needed to make to combine her home with Wyatt's. She just felt a simple, happy glow.

"Let's get started, then," said Wynona cheerfully as they walked into Beatrice's house. "I'll go over what I've planned and make sure it's exactly what you want."

Wynona quickly covered the simple arrangements she'd planned. The magnolias would be blooming and she showed them how she was planning on using the flowers and their great, waxy leaves as a backdrop to their ceremony and reception. As an accent to the large flowers, she planned some baby's breath arrangements in mason jars as a wispy accompaniment. They provided local appeal and a casual elegance that appealed to Beatrice.

"What do you think?" Beatrice asked Wyatt.

He smiled at her and held up his hands. "They look beautiful. But you know that my opinion on these things isn't worth very much. Despite all the years I've spent in churches around arrangements, my flower arranging knowledge is pretty pitiful. I know *I* like them."

"That's all we needed to know," said Wynona cheerfully as she closed her notebook. She hesitated and then asked, "Did I hear that you were both at the Nelmses' house when Caspian passed away?"

They nodded and Wynona continued, "How awful for you both. Was it one of the events celebrating the wedding?"

Beatrice sighed. "Sadly, yes."

"And I heard it was murder?" Wynona looked steadily at them.

Wyatt nodded. "I'm afraid so."

Wynona sighed. "That's terrible. And I feel so guilty."

Beatrice and Wyatt glanced at each other. Wyatt said gently to Wynona, "Why would you feel guilty about Caspian's death?"

Wynona gave a short laugh. "I guess because I've wanted it to happen for so long. Now that it *has* happened, I almost feel as if I've wished it on him somehow."

Beatrice said wryly, "I think the person responsible for his death is the person who murdered him. And that person *wasn't* you, from what I'm understanding?"

"Oh, I was nowhere near the house. That place gives me the creeps now—so many memories. Both good ones and bad ones," said Wynona quickly.

Beatrice said, "And you weren't on good terms with Caspian."

Wynona raised her eyebrows and then gave another short laugh. "Sometimes I forget that you're still relatively a newcomer to Dappled Hills, Beatrice. No, I was no friend of Caspian Nelms. I was dating Hawkins, his oldest child. We were in love, and the only thing I wanted in this whole world was to marry him."

"And Caspian disapproved," said Beatrice.

"Exactly," said Wynona.

"Why on earth did he disapprove? You're an attractive woman with her own business," said Beatrice. "It doesn't make any sense."

"He and my late-father never liked each other. When I was growing up, we lived next door to Caspian. There was a dispute over the property line that meant my father had to tear down a fence that he'd just paid for. And there was more than just that—the two men never seemed to get along over anything. Caspian took an instant dislike to me. Besides that, he'd wanted Hawkins to do something to make him proud—marry a debutante or a successful business woman or something. You know—some kind of advantageous marriage that would further his empire," said Wynona, a bitter note in her voice.

"A debutante? Here in Dappled Hills?" asked Beatrice.

"Well, I think the plan was for Hawkins to travel and find someone in New York or Dallas or something. Anyway, a poor woman with a small business from North Carolina wasn't part of the plan. Especially *me*. He forbade us to get married," said Wynona.

"That must have been incredibly upsetting," said Wyatt softly.

"It destroyed me," said Wynona simply. "At first, I just laughed it off. I told Hawkins I didn't care a thing about his money and that it would suit me just fine if we never saw his father again. But Hawkins relied on his father's money too much. He worried about being able to make a living without his father's support. And Caspian lowered the boom and said that if Hawkins married me, he would cut him completely off, financially. Hawkins didn't think he could make it."

"Did you get the impression that Hawkins needed money?" asked Beatrice.

Wynona nodded. "I did. And I didn't understand it. I mean, I'm scraping by, but I have enough money to live off of. But Hawkins seemed to think he needed much *more* than that."

"Do you think he had any debts or anything?" asked Beatrice. She remembered Malcolm saying that the gambling debts had accrued *after* Hawkins broke things off with Wynona, but there could be other debts.

Wynona shrugged. "That's one area we didn't discuss very much. Obviously, we should have."

Beatrice said slowly, "If Hawkins needed money so badly, do you think that he could somehow have been involved in his father's death?"

"Oh no!" said Wynona immediately, shaking her head. "Hawkins is a straight-arrow. He would never do something like that."

Beatrice and Wyatt exchanged looks again.

Beatrice said, "That's interesting. I didn't necessarily get the impression that Hawkins was like that. But sometimes first impressions can be deceiving."

"What was he like at the dinner party?" asked Wynona. "Before Caspian's death?"

"He was quiet. Unsmiling. He drank a lot," said Beatrice. "I didn't feel particularly welcomed."

Wynona rubbed her temple as if it was hurting. "You know, lately he's seemed very agitated. It's worried me. Even though I've been furious with Hawkins for dumping me, I still care a lot about him. I still love him, despite all his shortcomings." She turned to Wyatt. "Do you think you could drop by and check on him? I know he always had a lot of respect for you, even though he might not have shown it last night."

Wyatt nodded. "I'm planning on going by later to visit with the family. I'll be happy to have a word with Hawkins privately, if he wants to, when I'm there."

Beatrice said, "Do you have any idea who might have been behind Caspian's murder?"

Wynona glanced at them and then glanced away. "I hate to say it, but the way the murder was carried out was really distinctive, wasn't it? I mean, y'all were all there in the house. A party was going on. And someone slipped away and murdered Caspian in the middle of it all. I can definitely say that kind of brazen approach sounds like Malcolm. I mean—like I said, I hate to point the finger at someone, but it's more characteristic of Malcolm than really anyone else."

Wyatt frowned. "Didn't Malcolm and his father get along?"

Wynona said, "Malcolm, on the surface, seems to be one of those people who gets along with *everybody*. He's friendly and outgoing. He smiles a lot. And he had a pretty good relationship with his father, at least compared with everyone else in the house. But Malcolm and Caspian were not as close as he might want you to think. I heard them arguing pretty frequently."

"What were they arguing about?" asked Beatrice.

"Oh, life in general sometimes. And sometimes they argued over Della. I think Caspian was about as happy over Della as he was over me," said Wynona wryly. "After all, Della would have been Malcolm's *third* wife. I think Caspian thought that Malcolm was about to make another mistake." She stood up and gave Noo-noo a rub. "Well, I guess that's enough gossip from me today! Let me know if y'all have any questions about the flowers or anything else. I know it's going to be such a special day." She looked at Noo-noo. "Beatrice, I would love to get Noo-noo together with my puppy. Watson has so much energy right now and he would love a playdate with Noo-noo. She's so laid-back and sweet that they would be perfect together."

"Sounds good! Let's set that up soon," said Beatrice.

Beatrice walked Wynona out and then walked back in to sit next to Wyatt on the sofa. Noo-noo jumped up to sit between them, grinning.

Wyatt laughed. "I think somebody might be a little jealous. Next time, I'll have to come over with some special corgi treats."

"Just call her Green Eyes," said Beatrice with a smile. "Or maybe it's just that she wants to sit next to *both* of us." She grew serious again. "What do you think about all this?"

Wyatt sighed. "I hate to see it. Of course, it was sad losing Caspian. I started feeling that maybe his relationship with his family was turning a new leaf. After all, Sadie had returned to Dappled Hills and was trying to work things out with her father. And I thought that Caspian seemed more contented lately. It's made me very sad. It's made me especially sad that someone in his family or very close to him was the one who ended his life."

Beatrice said, "I know. And Wynona is right—it was really brazen of the person to do it while we were all here. I wonder if they thought that with all the distractions and in and out movement of a party that it would somehow provide a better cover for murder."

"It appears to have worked. I can't remember who was what when. I know there was a lot of motion, a lot of checking on things in the kitchen or going to get drinks. Maybe it made sense to commit the murder under those circumstances, after all," said Wyatt.

Beatrice said, "I've gotten to know the family a little better today. Meadow and I went up to the Nelms house thinking that we'd catch most of them there, but Hawkins was alone."

"How was he?" asked Wyatt. "I know Wynona said he's been bad for a while."

"His mind wasn't on our visit at all. He looked anxious and sort of faded. It makes him seem guilty somehow, even though that's not really fair. He was so absentminded that Meadow and I were worried that he wasn't going to remember to put the fried chicken dinner into the fridge," said Beatrice.

Wyatt said, "It may be the stress of Caspian's sudden death. And, if he wasn't doing well before, it could have been especially stressful for him."

"Have they contacted you about the funeral yet?" asked Beatrice.

Wyatt shook his head. "No, but that makes sense. After all, there is still likely some forensic work going on. The funeral will probably be delayed a little."

"Meadow and I ran into Malcolm and then Della downtown today," said Beatrice. "They were handling Caspian's death much better than Hawkins. At least, that's how it seemed. They said that they were taking a break from going over arrangements for the funeral. They're definitely thinking about what they're doing for the service, even if they haven't spoken with you yet."

Wyatt said, "I'll go by there in a few minutes and talk to them."

"Between wedding flowers and funeral arrangements, you're having a busy day," said Beatrice ruefully.

"No busier than usual," said Wyatt cheerfully. "And talking about flower arrangements doesn't exactly qualify as work."

He put an arm around Beatrice and they sat in a happy glow for a few minutes. "It makes it seem more real, doesn't it?" asked Beatrice. "Getting the details hammered out for the ceremony."

"It certainly does," agreed Wyatt. He paused. "I was thinking that maybe we should do something—just the two of us. Our friends have been great to show their friendship with these different events, but it might be nice for us to celebrate our upcoming wedding in a quieter way."

Beatrice said, "That would be wonderful! I think I need to recharge a little after all the social events. What were you thinking?"

"I was thinking that we could take a hike up Sunset Mountain and have a picnic. The hike isn't too strenuous and the views and waterfalls are gorgeous. I know you enjoyed it up there the last couple of times we went. Only if that sounds good to you," said Wyatt quickly. "It's just that, if we do something in town, we'll have friends stopping by our table and visiting with us."

"That's the truth!" said Beatrice. "One of the joys—and hazards—of living in a small town. You never really get a *private* dinner, especially if you're a minister."

"Then it's a plan. Would tomorrow work for you?"

"Tomorrow would be perfect," said Beatrice with a smile.

Chapter Eight

After Wyatt left, Beatrice decided to put her feet up for a little while. Despite her nap earlier, she still felt tired. She headed into the backyard with Noo-noo and her book and climbed up into the hammock. She tossed Noo-noo a chew toy. She opened *Moby Dick* ... and fell promptly asleep.

Beatrice awoke with a jerk some time later, feeling very confused. Her cell phone was ringing in her pocket and Noo-noo was staring at her with a concerned expression. She fumbled with the phone, finally answering it.

It was Sadie Nelms on the phone.

"Did I wake you up?" Sadie asked with concern.

"Oh no, no," said Beatrice quickly, although she never quite knew exactly why she was so desperate to cover up the fact that she sometimes succumbed to an occasional nap. "No, it's just allergies, that's all. How are you doing? I'm so sorry about last night." She struggled to swing her legs out of the hammock so that she could sit up. She raised her hand to smooth down her hair.

"It's been a hard day," said Sadie frankly. "Of course, last night was such a terrible shock. And then—well, we're part of the investigation, naturally. Although I'm still clinging to the hope that somebody walked into the house and killed Father. The alternative is pretty difficult to face."

"Yes, I'm sure it would be," said Beatrice. She cleared her throat. "Have you ... well, can I help in any way? Hawkins may have mentioned that Meadow and I stopped by earlier. Meadow made some food that smelled delicious. I could help with an obituary or bring in more food, or come by with Wyatt?" She felt she was just flinging possibilities out there, but she hated telling people 'let me know how I can help'. It seemed kinder to offer some ways *to* help.

Sadie said, "Yes, and that's one reason I wanted to call—to thank you for the food. It's such a load off my mind not to have to think about cooking tonight."

"Oh good. And, well, you know that was Meadow's doing, right? My cooking is usually competent, but nothing to write home about," said Beatrice. "Although I could make you an *excellent* breakfast."

Sadie laughed. "I appreciate your coming by anyway. As I mentioned, it's been a hard day. I think we've figured out the details for my father's service and obituary, though. At least—I have. Somehow it seems to fall to the daughter to do this stuff."

"Is there any part left that I can help with? I could be the go-between for you and Wyatt, if you've got the service planned. I'll be seeing him, after all," she said with a laugh. "Although he did say that he was coming by to see you—or at least will be contacting you to set up a time."

Sadie said, "And it's not like you both don't have enough on your plate trying to plan a wedding!" She hesitated. "Actually, there is something you can do. I have a feeling that, even though I'm the one who set up all the plans for the service, if I'm just giving Wyatt the outline for it that Malcolm or Hawkins might object to my choices. It would be great to have another woman to back me up and say that the choices of Bible verse and hymn and whatever were good ones. And, since it's Wyatt, maybe you wouldn't feel too awkward doing that?"

"Consider it done," said Beatrice quickly. "And I need to get used to accompanying him on various church business anyway. What time would work for you?"

"How about late morning tomorrow?" asked Sadie. "That way hopefully everyone will be awake but no one will have left yet." She paused. "And if Hawkins isn't awake, I'll be sure to wake him up."

"Is Hawkins all right?" asked Beatrice. "When I was there this morning, he seemed to be taking your father's death pretty hard."

Sadie gave a hard laugh. "I don't know what's happening to Hawkins. I certainly don't think that he's really upset about Father's death. How could he be, when they argued all the time?"

"Maybe he feels guilty about the arguing now that his father is gone," said Beatrice slowly.

"I guess it's possible. Still, he should have thought about that while Father was still alive," said Sadie briskly. "All right ... so ... tomorrow morning?"

"I'll see you then," said Beatrice.

After she got off the phone with Sadie, she called Wyatt to let him know about the plans to go over Caspian's funeral service. With any luck, they would still be able to get away relatively early for their hike and picnic. Then she gave *Moby Dick* a rueful look. It just wasn't the right time to read the story and she knew it. She knew it must be one of Ramsay's favorite books because it was covered in marginalia. Ramsay had added notes and comments in different pens during different readings. The more she thought about it, the more she thought she should give it back to him and tell him she'd try it again another time.

Beatrice briefly called Meadow to make sure she was home.

"I'm here! Ramsay isn't, though. No worries—I'll make sure he gets his precious book back. I know how he loves that thing," said Meadow.

"I'll be there in a minute," said Beatrice. "I think I'll let Noo-noo stretch her legs one more time today before it gets dark."

She put the corgi on her leash, grabbed the book, and they headed out the door.

The sun was setting and the reds and purples and oranges in the sky were beautiful against the backdrop of trees. Noo-noo took off at a leisurely pace, stopping frequently to smell things.

On the short walk over, a small, red car stopped, and the driver, a briskly efficient-looking woman in her fifties, gave Beatrice a cheery smile as she rolled down the window.

Beatrice frantically tried to remember the woman's name. She knew that she was very involved in Wyatt's church (*our* church, she reminded herself). She'd never thought of herself as someone who had a hard time remembering names, but moving to a new town meant learning dozens of them. She hesitated. Charlene. Surely she was Charlene.

Beatrice said, "Hi, Charlene! Beautiful afternoon, isn't it?"

The woman's smile was wide, but just a bit on the brittle side. *Not* Charlene, decided Beatrice.

"It's Char-*maine* , actually," said the woman. "But you were close. I'm glad to run into you, Beatrice. I've been thinking about you and Wyatt and your upcoming wedding. You must be frantically busy right now, trying to finish up the last-minute details! Your wedding is the hottest ticket in town right now, you know." She grinned again, but it didn't quite reach her eyes.

"I'm sorry? Hottest ticket ... what?" Beatrice knew herself to be a smart and educated woman, but right now she felt super-slow. What was Charmaine trying to get at? Or was she getting at anything at all?

"I mean that not everyone can get in. I didn't get an invitation, myself," said Charmaine, with a short laugh. "Although everyone thinks I did, since I spend *so* much time at the church."

Beatrice was annoyed to find herself flushing. "That's because we're only having family and the closest of our friends. It's a second wedding for both of us, and we just wanted to keep the celebration very intimate. You understand." Although Beatrice wasn't at all sure that Charmaine did. Charmaine was likely one of those brides who had twelve bridesmaids and twelve groomsmen at her wedding.

"I see. Well, that's not really what I wanted to talk to you about. I mainly wanted to see what you were planning on doing at the church." Charmaine leaned a bit farther on her car window as if dying to hear what Beatrice was about to say.

Beatrice again wondered if her brain simply wasn't operating at capacity today. "Sorry? Planning on doing at the church?"

Now Charmaine looked impatient. "You know—you'll be the preacher's wife. I do a lot of things at the church and I'm happy to stop doing some of them if you'd like to take over." Since Beatrice wasn't immediately answering, Charmaine continued, "Like altar guild, if you're good at arranging flowers. Or maybe you're looking for an activity like the choir or handbells."

Beatrice blinked. She was pretty sure that she wasn't looking for an activity like choir or handbells, not being musically-inclined at all. But now, at least, she knew what Charmaine was getting at. She was about to be the minister's wife and there were going to be some members of the congregation that would expect her to take more of a public role in the church.

"I'm still mulling it over," said Beatrice truthfully. The fact that she'd just *started* mulling it over was something that she wouldn't share with Charmaine.

"All right," said Charmaine, a bit begrudgingly. "Let me know if you need any more information on ways to serve." And she drove speedily away.

When she and Noo-noo reached Meadow's house, a car pulled up in the driveway behind Beatrice. She turned and smiled. Ramsay had gotten back home. Beatrice felt better about handing off the book to him personally. Considering that their dog, Boris, ate just about everything in sight, she'd like to make sure to put the book right into Ramsay's hands.

Ramsay climbed out of his police cruiser and waved a hand at Beatrice. She saw that the sharp lines in his face stood out, and that Ramsay looked like he needed to crawl into the bed. When he caught sight of his book, though, he suddenly became more animated.

"Read it already?" he asked, a smile tugging at his lips. "Or did you decide to give up?"

"Not give up, but temporarily *retreat* from *Moby Dick*," said Beatrice, grinning at him. "I'm not sure what I was thinking. I'm in the final stages of wedding planning, for heaven's sake."

"Well, I sort of wondered about that, but you seemed game enough," said Ramsay, chuckling as he took the book back. He thumbed through the pages affectionately. "Maybe it would be good for me if I started reading it again. Especially now." He made a face.

"Case getting you down?" asked Beatrice.

"In a way. It's tough investigating the family, even though in all likelihood, it *is* a member of the family responsible. They're naturally reluctant to answer questions, and they seem to think I can make this all go away, since I'm police chief and a friend of the family. I've had to explain that's not the way it works."

"Did forensics come back with a cause of death?" asked Beatrice.

Ramsay gave a grim nod. "It was as I thought—death by smothering. The sleeping pills administered in his drink certainly helped. And Caspian could be counted on to have an afternoon cocktail and a nap."

"But why on earth murder him when everyone was there?" asked Beatrice.

Ramsay shrugged. "Sheer brashness. And cockiness. An over-confidence that the killer thought he could get away with it." Noo-noo nudged Ramsay with her nose and he bent to rub the little dog.

"Do those characteristics seem to point to one member of the family over another?" asked Beatrice. "I still don't know them very well, even though they were holding a party on my behalf."

Ramsay said, "Well, that's tricky. Of course, the family member who immediately comes to mind is Malcolm. But that's only because he's such an extrovert. I don't think the rest of the family suffers from lack of confidence, either."

Beatrice asked slowly, "I was talking with Wynona today and she was asking a lot of questions about what happened. You know—she's helping with some of my wedding arrangements."

Ramsay nodded. "And you think that she seems awfully interested, considering she's no longer dating Hawkins. Or engaged to him, or whatever kind of an arrangement they had. Unfortunately, considering their history, the very public nature of their breakup, and the fact that Wynona has been furious at Caspian for years, I have to keep her in mind for possible involvement."

Beatrice asked, "Is there any particular reason that you are? Was she seen there? She told Wyatt and me that she wasn't anywhere near the Nelms estate at the time of Caspian's death."

"Not because of any evidence, but just because of the circumstances. And, let's be honest, the house was hardly a fortress that night. The doors were all unlocked and a couple of windows were wide open while we were there. The groundskeeper was in and out. The place was like a sieve," Ramsay said, looking frustrated.

"I'm sure you'll figure it out," said Beatrice. "It's only a matter of time."

Ramsay said, "I know you're not officially on the Dappled Hills police force, but you seem to have a knack for figuring these types of things out, Beatrice. If you hear anything or even just get a gut feeling about something, please let me know." He gave a dry laugh. "Maybe, in essence, I've basically just handed another *Moby Dick* to you. You just got finished telling me how you didn't have any time before your big day."

"Oh, I think I have time to keep an ear out. And I will, Ramsay, of course." Beatrice glanced up at the barn that served as Ramsay's home. "Now you should go on inside and let Meadow stuff you with her good cooking until you can fall asleep. Tell her you caught up with me outside so she won't think I've been murdered on the way to her house," she said lightly.

Ramsay nodded, already heading off in that direction. "Thanks!" he said, raising *Moby Dick* in the air as he hurried for food and sleep.

Around 10:30 the next morning, Wyatt tapped on Beatrice's door. He had a picnic basket in hand.

She let him in with a smile. "I'm just clearing away the breakfast dishes. I'll be done in a jiff. I seem to be running behind today with my cleaning, even though I was up so early. Miss Sissy was lurking in my azalea bushes again and Noo-noo let me know about it. Plus the fact that the poor dog across the woods was barking the better part of the night. I finally just gave up sleeping."

"No sign of Maisie yet?" asked Wyatt, setting down the picnic basket and drying off a glass for her.

"Not a glimpse of her. At least I got Miss Sissy to have some food before she went back out to search. I told her I'd help her later. I have the feeling that she's spending the whole day looking for that cat. But Maisie might be scared and hiding still—she's not used to being outside, after all. The cat could be totally fine and just determined to keep out of sight," said Beatrice. She glanced over Wyatt and smiled, "You look awfully nice for a hike."

Wyatt looked down at his khaki pants and button-down shirt and laughed. "I didn't want to go over the funeral arrangements while wearing jeans. I guess it won't be too strenuous of a hike."

"Definitely not with what you're wearing!" She picked up her purse.

Wyatt looked concerned. "About looking for Maisie—I wish I could help you out. I've got hospital visits in Lenoir later this afternoon, though."

They walked out the door and into Wyatt's car. "Oh, no worries. I plan on roping Meadow into searching. She'll probably be good at flushing Maisie out of the undergrowth," said Beatrice with a smile. Meadow could be loud and animated. Any skittish cat would be sure to run. "Now, about this funeral. It sounds like planning the service could be tricky."

Wyatt nodded as he pulled out of the driveway. "Sometimes it's like that. Families want to make the service perfect and they'll have different ideas about how to make it perfect."

"I think that's the kind of situation we're heading for," said Beatrice grimly. "I promised Sadie that I'd support her in her choices of hymn, Bible verse, or whatever."

Wyatt said, "Do whatever you need to do. I'm not really in a good position to offer an opinion. I'll have to be neutral if the siblings start arguing about the service."

Beatrice heaved a large sigh. "I hope it doesn't devolve into that. That would be really sad—arguing over their father's funeral."

Wyatt pulled into the circular driveway in front of the Nelms house and parked in the shade under a large tree overhanging the driveway. Beatrice saw the groundskeeper, Barkis, as she was getting out of the car. He was working on an ancient, tractor-style lawnmower. He spat out a stream of tobacco when he spotted her and turned his attention back on his repairs.

Sadie answered the door immediately. She was wearing black Capri pants and a crisp white blouse. "Thank you both for coming over," she said quietly, shaking their hands. "I've managed to get everyone somewhat settled in the drawing room."

It wasn't a very happy-looking bunch, decided Beatrice, although to be fair, there wasn't much to be happy about. Hawkins slouched on a silk sofa, looking as if he wanted to pick a fight. Beatrice supposed that was a slight improvement on the previous visit when he looked as if he was off in space. Malcolm stood up, grinned at them, and shook their hands but then resumed a rather wary expression. Surprisingly, Della was there. Beatrice had thought that most likely it would only be family attending. Maybe she was just present to offer Malcolm moral support.

Della, as if sensing Beatrice's thoughts, quickly said, "I'll go bring some iced tea and give y'all a chance to talk."

Malcolm quickly said, "Iced tea would be great, but then come back to us. I'd like to hear your opinion, too."

This made both Sadie and Hawkins scowl. Sadie looked as if the last thing in the world that she wanted to hear was another opinion. Hawkins seemed to be unhappily reflecting on something—maybe regretting that he'd ended his relationship with Wynona when Malcolm and Della seemed to be so happy together. Beatrice wondered if Hawkins did still have feelings for Wynona. He certainly wasn't dating anyone else, so maybe he did still hold a torch for her.

Della scooted out, heading to the kitchen for the tea. Sadie immediately launched into her plans, as if determined to outline them before Della could weigh in.

Wyatt nodded, taking notes as Sadie talked. Beatrice dutifully interjected murmurs of 'excellent' and 'good choice' when Sadie mentioned "How Great Thou Art" as the hymn and Psalm 23 for the verse. In her head, she was wondering how anyone could really disagree with those extremely traditional choices.

Beatrice found out a moment later when Hawkins said, "I don't like it."

Sadie took a deep breath and took a long look at the ceiling as if her patience might be found up there somewhere. "What's not to like about 'The Lord is my Shepherd?'"

"Father wouldn't like it. He'd want something a little more modern," insisted Hawkins.

Sadie said incredulously, "Are you talking about *Caspian Nelms*? Or do you have a different father? Because I'm pretty sure that Caspian Nelms was about as traditional as they came. Besides, the service is to please the living, not the dead."

"Even more reason for us to go with something more modern," said Hawkins. "Because I don't like either choice. And I'd like more input."

Sadie gave Beatrice a pleading look and Beatrice cleared her throat. The last thing she wanted to do was to get involved in this squabble, but she'd promised Sadie that she'd help. She said slowly, "I'm sure there's room for a compromise. Why not have a slightly longer service and have one traditional hymn and one more modern choice? And the same thing with the scripture ... although I'm not sure there's a modern choice for scripture." She gave a short laugh.

"We could do a modern meditation from a Bible scholar," said Malcolm in a mending-fences way.

Wyatt sat, pencil poised over the paper and a thoughtful expression on his face.

Finally, after some hot words and a bit more squabbling, they decided to compromise on the service and do a little of everything. Wyatt said that he would help find selections for a modern meditation.

Hawkins said goodbye to Wyatt and Beatrice and disappeared. Malcolm did the same a few minutes later, giving them a cheerful goodbye as he left. Sadie grimaced at Beatrice as they were left alone.

Chapter Nine

"Thanks for helping with that ... both of you. I guess a compromise did make more sense, especially if it meant saving the peace," said Sadie.

Wyatt said, "It's easy enough to mix the style of a service." He gently asked, "How are you doing?"

Somehow, his gentleness seemed to be the emotional undoing of Sadie. A few tears trickled down her cheeks and she brushed them impatiently away. "I'm fine—ignore the evidence of the tears," she said dryly. "It's just that I'm totally exhausted. I haven't slept the last couple of nights at all. And now I don't want anything to do with sleeping pills." She gave a harsh laugh.

Beatrice nodded. "I spoke briefly with Ramsay and he mentioned that your father's drink had been doctored. I'm so sorry."

Sadie said, "What's more, it's terrible knowing that I'm living in a house with a murderer. That definitely doesn't help with the insomnia. I'm thinking I know who's responsible, too."

Beatrice and Wyatt exchanged worried glances.

Then Sadie waved her hand in the air. "But I don't have any proof. I won't destroy this family any more than it already has been with empty allegations and no evidence. I just can't believe what's happened. Here I was, at home, trying to mend fences with Father before it was too late. And I'm not really sure that we ever saw things on the same page."

They heard the sound of decisive footsteps coming from the direction of the kitchen. A smile twisted Sadie's lips. "I have a feeling that Della has gone far beyond the recommended iced tea. She can't seem to help herself from entertaining."

Sadie was right. Della came into the drawing room with a large tray loaded with glasses of iced tea, a plate of cookies, and some cheese and crackers.

"Sorry about the delay," she said cheerily. "I guess I got carried away." Della looked around. "Where did everybody go?"

Wyatt said, "We've already settled on a service, Della. But your snacks look delicious."

Della's eyes widened. "Really? You've figured out the hymns and stuff already? Wow. I thought you were going to be here all day."

Sadie said wryly, "Apparently compromise is the quickest way to resolve disputes. Who knew?"

Della said with a laugh, "Well, I hope you'll stay for a few minutes and help me eat all this." She set the tray down on a large ottoman near their chairs and watched as Beatrice and Wyatt each took a small plate and filled it with refreshments.

Sadie seemed irritated with Della and wasn't making any conversation so Beatrice decided to try and fill the sudden silence. She cleared her throat. "Sadie, Meadow says you make lovely quilts. Are you in the Cut-Ups guild?"

Sadie shook her head. "You know, I've never really been part of a guild. I was interested in it before moving away, but then when I left I never joined one. I never stopped quilting, though." She looked thoughtful. "You know, this would actually be a great time to join up. I need some distraction from what's going on in my personal life and I could use some fresh ideas and input from other quilters."

"I hope you'll consider joining the Village Quilters," said Beatrice with a smile. "You know how thrilled Meadow would be."

Wyatt said, "Meadow would be over the moon. And it's a great group of women—very involved in the community."

Sadie was looking at Della, though, and Beatrice thought she detected a touch of malice in her gaze. "Della, I think we should both visit the Village Quilters guild."

"What?" Della looked startled and irritated and Beatrice realized that she'd been miles away in her head and not really listening to Sadie or Beatrice at all.

Sadie raised her voice as if Della was having trouble hearing her. "I said that you and I will go visit the Village Quilters at their next guild meeting, which is … ?" She looked expectantly at Beatrice.

Beatrice thought for a second. "As a matter of fact, the next guild meeting is tomorrow. I've been so busy I don't think it was even on my radar. Good thing we're talking about it now. And we'd love to have you both come."

Della stared at Sadie. "I don't think I'm ready to be part of a guild."

"We're just *visiting*. I didn't say that you needed to *join*. Besides, don't you want to improve your quilting?" asked Sadie.

There was an almost sarcastic tone to Sadie's voice. Della definitely seemed to pick up on it and bristled.

"I do want to improve it. But it takes time. I'm still trying to gather together supplies and figure out what kind of beginner's quilt I should start on," said Della, sounding defensive.

"All the better to go to a guild meeting. I'm sure the ladies there will have tons of advice and ideas for you," said Sadie.

"Yes." Della looked doubtful at this eventuality. She stood up. "Well, I'd better check in with Malcolm. I think he said that we had some errands to run this afternoon. Good to see you Beatrice and Wyatt."

She left without looking back at Sadie.

Sadie made a face behind her back. "Good riddance." She glanced over at Wyatt and seemed slightly abashed. "Sorry. I know I was behaving badly. But I just feel like Della is spinning her wheels. I don't think she's interested in quilting at all."

Beatrice frowned. "But she's spending a lot of time and money in the Patchwork Cottage."

Sadie shrugged. "I think it's all for show. Malcolm, believe it or not, is a very old-fashioned guy. And I think Della is fashioning *herself* to fit his idea of the ideal woman. She's been as crafty as she possibly can be and that's in response to Malcolm expressing admiration for women who could sew or crochet or quilt."

Wyatt frowned and asked in a quiet voice, "So she didn't knit or do any other sewing before he said that?"

"Oh, I think she *did*. But I don't think she did nearly as much of it. Plus, she's just expanding into quilting to please him. Our mother quilted and he always admired the craft. It'll serve Della right to go to a guild meeting," said Sadie. Then she laughed. "I know I must sound awful, but I just get tired of it."

Beatrice and Wyatt glanced at each other and stood up. Beatrice said, "Well, we'll look forward to seeing you both at the guild meeting tomorrow. And I think Wyatt and I should be on our way. I know you've got tons to do."

They made their goodbyes, and then Beatrice and Wyatt got back in Wyatt's car. Beatrice said, "Whew. It's exhausting dealing with that family. I don't know how you do it."

Wyatt laughed. "They're not *that* bad. It's just a stressful time for them and they're having to deal with family at the same time."

"I mean, I don't know how you deal with this *all the time*. Because you're always dealing with people in stressful circumstances: a birth, a death, a wedding, an illness. I wish I had half the patience that you do," said Beatrice.

"I think you're more patient than you think," said Wyatt.

Beatrice gave him a rueful look. "And I think you might be looking at me through rose-colored glasses. Although maybe your patience is rubbing off on me a little bit. With any luck, that will continue."

Wyatt gave her a teasing look. "You think I might strain your ability to be patient?"

"No, but I have the feeling that combining our two households might. Don't you think it's going to be tricky?" asked Beatrice.

Wyatt grinned and said lightly, "The fact that we both have small houses and we're trying to move one household into another? What could be tricky?" He pulled into the parking lot for the trail and picnic area.

"Are you sure that my cottage is slightly roomier than the parsonage? I've never particularly thought of it as being roomy before," said Beatrice.

"I wouldn't say it was *roomy*, but I think we'll have enough room. It will just be cozy. If we find that we don't have the space for everything, I'm sure there are lots of things that I can give away at the church yard sale," said Wyatt.

Beatrice felt a little abashed. Wyatt had already gone through his things at least once or twice, winnowing his possessions down to the bare minimum. She cleared her throat. "I have a confession to make."

"I'm a Presbyterian minister, not a priest," said Wyatt with a twinkle in his eye.

"At any rate, I have a confession. I know that I've still got boxes from my previous move from Atlanta to Dappled Hills. They ... um ... haven't been unpacked yet and are in my tiny attic." Beatrice had the grace to blush.

Wyatt said, "Now I'm curious. What's in the mysterious boxes?"

"Apparently very important things! That I haven't needed in years. All right, I think I'm inspired. I'm going to take Noo-noo for a quick walk, and then I'm going to start doing some serious cleaning," said Beatrice.

"Don't give anything away that you'll regret later," said Wyatt, looking concerned.

"Oh, no worries—I won't. But I have the feeling that the things I'll be coming across aren't sentimental items. They might be tools from the old house that I don't need or old clothes that don't fit." She got out of the car and smiled at Wyatt. "I'll let you know what I uncover."

Fortunately, it was a day of low-humidity and Wyatt didn't seem at all uncomfortable in his khakis and button-down during their hike. They passed a beautiful waterfall with cascades that sent a cooling mist their way. Wyatt put their picnic down on a picnic table in a shady spot where they could still see the waterfall—but not so close that the sound of the water drowned out their voices.

After they enjoyed their chicken salad sandwiches, deviled eggs, and cantaloupe, Beatrice said thoughtfully, "I ran into Charlene today."

Wyatt looked puzzled and Beatrice quickly corrected herself. "I mean *Charmaine*. I can't seem to get her name right, which is certainly not helping me become very popular with her. I understand that she does a lot at the church."

Wyatt nodded, wiping his fingers off carefully with a checkered cotton napkin. "That she does. Sometimes I think that we'd have to have ten volunteers to take Charmaine's place if she stopped volunteering."

"Charmaine suggested that I might want to take over some volunteer roles at the church," said Beatrice with a frown.

Wyatt looked concerned and then Beatrice amended it to, "Well, she didn't really *suggest* it. She sort of assumed that I would want to be more actively involved. Charmaine suggested altar guild and the choir."

She stopped to gauge Wyatt's response to this.

He was quiet for a moment and then said thoughtfully, "I don't remember your being very interested in singing at the church before."

"Heavens, no. My voice would likely make the congregation take flight from the sanctuary," said Beatrice fervently.

"And I don't remember your having a lifelong dream to be involved in altar guild or vacation Bible school, or to be a church pianist, organist, or cook," he said slowly.

"Not in this lifetime, at any rate," said Beatrice, already feeling relieved. "But I would like to spend more time at church—and a big reason, besides having a greater spiritual connection, would be to spend more time with you. My choice would likely include volunteer work. I like to visit retirement homes or help in the community. It would make me feel as if I'm making more of a contribution."

Wyatt reached out and held her hand. "I didn't decide to marry you in order to recruit another volunteer for the church. I want you to do what feels right to *you*. I think your role, and my role, in our marriage is to provide a loving home for each other."

For the next few minutes, they embraced with the cascading waterfalls providing a beautiful backdrop.

After the picnic, Wyatt took Beatrice back home. She felt, as usual, relaxed and recharged after spending time with him. Recharged enough to finally tackle the clutter she'd collected in the past decades. For the next couple of hours, Beatrice explored tiny closets, her tiny attic, and tiny cabinets and drawers. She found that she'd managed to squirrel away a large number of unnecessary items. She also found that she'd stirred up a good deal of dust. Beatrice was giving her third tremendous sneeze in a row when there was a light tap at her front door.

Beatrice made a face. She wasn't exactly looking like she was ready for a visit. She pushed strands of hair out of her eyes. There was dust and streaks of dirt on the front of her button-down shirt and khaki capris. She'd been so inspired to start her project that she'd forgotten to change into older clothes before starting it.

Beatrice peered out of her front window and saw Meadow grinning back at her. She relaxed. Meadow wasn't the kind of company that one had to dress up for.

But it was important to give even Meadow a place to sit. As Meadow walked in, she gave a low whistle. "Boy, Beatrice! You've been doing some work!"

And indeed, just about every available surface was covered with ... stuff. There were old boxes, extra clothes hangers, craft supplies she no longer needed, clothes that didn't fit or were out of style or had never really been worn, and books she'd inherited from earlier generations that hadn't been read.

Beatrice smiled at Meadow. "I'm glad that *that* was your immediate reaction, instead of 'what a mess!' Because looking around right now, all I'm really seeing is the mess. The mess on the chairs and tables and the mess on me!"

Meadow shook her head and waved her hand in a dismissive gesture. "Don't you know that the only way to really clean is to make everything look worse before it looks better? No, this is awesome! Is it sorted?"

"Sorted? I guess it is, in a way. I tried to keep the trash in that corner over there. Everything else has got to be given away. And, if I wanted to keep something, I just put it back where I found it as I was working through the closets and attic," said Beatrice.

Meadow nodded, looking impressed. "You've gotten a ton done. I'm guessing this is in anticipation of Wyatt moving in?"

"That's right. He was being very generous about offering to pare down his possessions to move in." Beatrice laughed. "But I don't think he has a ton of possessions to begin with! I figured I'd better sort through my own junk to make room for his things. Anyway, I'm sure this isn't what you came here to talk about."

Meadow said, "You're right about that. But there's nowhere to sit! And this is a lot of stuff to give away by yourself. I'll give you a hand."

Beatrice protested, "You don't have any time to spend working on something like this!"

"On the contrary! This will be the perfect distraction. I've been trying to make phone calls for Ash and Piper to compare caterers. I've talked to enough people that my head is spinning now. This is a great way to un-spin it," said Meadow cheerfully. "Why don't you take on the trash and I'll load my van with the stuff you want to give away. Then we'll head to the Goodwill and unload it."

Beatrice had to admit that it was much easier with someone else helping. The problem with organizing is that by the time you've pulled everything out and sorted it, you're completely exhausted. Then there's the trash and give away piles to deal with when you have no energy to address it. Meadow was speedy and cheerful and they got everything cleared out in no time.

They were in Meadow's van on the way to the Goodwill to donate the unwanted items, when Meadow said, "You're coming to the guild meeting tomorrow, aren't you? It's actually at my house this time. I've got some new ideas for volunteer projects and we'll need a quorum to vote on them."

"I'll be there," said Beatrice, gripping the door as Meadow sped down the road. Meadow's driving, particularly when she was engaged in conversation, was enough to get her heart thumping. "I'll admit I'd forgotten about it at first, with everything going on. But I realized earlier today that it was tomorrow. And you'll be proud of me—I actually recruited a couple of people to come."

Meadow looked surprised, and then Beatrice thought she spotted the merest bit of consternation on her face before she grinned at her. "We'll have to promote you to membership chairman! Who did you get to visit?"

"I guess technically I only recruited Sadie to visit and then Sadie recruited Della," said Beatrice. "But they're both supposed to be coming."

"Great!" said Meadow. "I'll give them a call since I'm hosting and give them the scoop. We'll put out the red carpet for them. And you'll *definitely* be there? Despite all the craziness and the events, and all?"

"I've got a quilt that I've been working on for months now and I really haven't gotten anywhere with it. Every time I pick it up, it seems like I have to put it down again just a couple of minutes later. I haven't even had enough time to figure out where I left off," said Beatrice as Meadow pulled into the Goodwill.

Meadow said in a considering way, "Is it something you were planning to work on at the meeting?"

"Probably not—it's a machine quilt. I'm just planning on getting inspiration from everybody else's progress and maybe transfer it to mine when I get home," said Beatrice wryly.

"That's just as well. Since we need to vote on the volunteering and all," said Meadow.

Beatrice made a face. "It's going to be mainly a business meeting? That's too bad—I was hoping that I could give Sadie more of an overview of how the Village Quilters really operates."

"Oh, I'm sure she'll see how much fun we have. And we'll be sure to talk about our current projects and all," said Meadow in a rush. "And don't you mean Sadie *and* Della?"

Beatrice said, "I suppose I do, although Sadie seems to think that Della really isn't all that interested in quilting at all."

"Not interested in quilting!" said Meadow indignantly. "How on earth could that be? She spends a lot of money over at the Patchwork Cottage. And she's always talking about quilting whenever I see her."

Beatrice shrugged as they climbed out of the van and opened the trunk. "Sadie seemed to think Della was putting on some sort of an act for Malcolm's benefit. She said that Malcolm is a lot more old-fashioned than he looks and he really appreciates all the old crafts and that sort of thing. Sadie made it sound like Della is trying to hook Malcolm."

Meadow made a considering face. "Well, I suppose he is a big catch, isn't he? Maybe it's worth trying to pick up an extra hobby. She's definitely *crafty*, I can see that. She's shown me some of the things that she's made and I've been quite impressed. Della isn't faking *that*."

The next few minutes were spent helping the Goodwill worker unload Meadow's van of all of Beatrice's superfluous possessions. Beatrice took her receipt and they got back in the car.

Meadow beamed at her as she started driving off again at her breakneck pace. "Now, don't you feel better? Getting rid of all that extra stuff? Doesn't it make you feel freer, somehow?"

Beatrice sighed. "I feel a little conflicted. In some ways, I feel like I've done a great job getting rid of things that I probably would never need again. But in some ways, I worry that I'm going to need one of the things that I just gave away—probably immediately."

Meadow waved her hand in the air. "Then you'll just buy it—a more recent, probably improved thing."

"I know you're right," said Beatrice. "And yes, in a lot of ways I *do* feel productive. After all, I got a lot of things accomplished today."

"Which is part of why I wanted to talk to you," said Meadow. "Your *productivity*. Especially when talking to our suspects. How did your time with Wynona go?"

"Wynona asked a lot of questions. Of course, she said that she wasn't anywhere near the Nelms house when Caspian died," said Beatrice.

Meadow said, "Who did she think might be responsible for Caspian's death?"

Beatrice winced as Meadow continued looking at her with a furrowed brow. "Meadow, the road!"

Meadow quickly returned her attention to the road, just in time to swerve around a large branch that had fallen in the middle of the street. "Sorry. So, what did she think?"

Beatrice said, "I don't really know how she could even hazard a good guess. After all, she wasn't there. She hadn't seen the family dynamics at work. And she hasn't dated Hawkins for a while."

Meadow said, "That's true, but she knows the family *really* well. Of course, Sadie wasn't around at the time, but Wynona has become good friends with her since she's moved back home. I think she'd have very good instincts for who could have done such a thing."

"In that case, her answer was Malcolm," said Beatrice.

Meadow exclaimed, "Malcolm! Wow. He seems like the best-adjusted one out of the whole bunch. Charming. And cute, too. Not that anyone could pull me away from my wonderful Ramsay, of course."

"Wynona said that Malcolm *seems* to be well-adjusted and outgoing, but that he and his father had their disagreements. Wynona said that she had heard Malcolm and Caspian argue a few times," said Beatrice.

"I can't imagine what about," said Meadow. "Malcolm actually has a well-paying job, unlike Hawkins. Surely he didn't argue with his father over money."

"Not over money, apparently. Wynona said she heard Malcolm arguing with Caspian over Della. She said that Caspian wasn't very pleased with Malcolm's choice in Della," said Beatrice.

"Caspian wouldn't know a good candidate for marriage if it hit him in the face!" Meadow waved both hands in the air to punctuate her statement and temporarily drove on the other side of the road before quickly regaining control of the car. "After all, he didn't exactly make a good match himself, did he? His own wife left him. Or he left her … whatever. I can't remember all the details. Anyway, there's nothing wrong with Wynona or Della."

Beatrice said, "Wynona is still upset over it, too. She said that she still loves Hawkins, 'despite all his shortcomings.' So she knows he's got issues."

"But she didn't think that he could murder Caspian? Even though he clearly needed the money?" asked Meadow, pulling into Beatrice's driveway.

Beatrice gave a sigh of relief at finally being parked and safe from Meadow's erratic driving. Meadow was starting to drive more like Miss Sissy every day. "No. And besides, she said that the crime was very distinctive—sort of brazen. She thinks that Malcolm fits the bill a lot more than Hawkins."

"I can imagine that," said Meadow. "Hawkins was sort of vague and absentminded when we were dropping off the chicken. He sure didn't seem like a criminal mastermind. Unless the reason he was acting the way he was is because he was feeling guilty over murdering his father."

Beatrice said, "Wynona also said that Caspian didn't like her because he held a grudge against her late-father."

Meadow snapped her fingers. "That's right. I'd forgotten about that. Some sort of property dispute. Although it seems kind of silly to hold something like that against Wynona. She was just a kid at the time. Caspian was pretty stubborn, though. Okay, then, so that's Wynona. Did you talk with anyone else?"

Beatrice saw Noo-noo grinning at her from the front window. She gave a wave to the little dog and then felt a bit foolish. Do dogs understand waves? Beatrice said absently to Meadow, "As a matter of fact, Sadie called me up—sort of out of the blue. She thought that there was going to be something of a family scuffle over the service."

Meadow gaped at her. "What? A scuffle at the funeral service?"

"No, no. A scuffle while *planning* the service. And I'm exaggerating—she thought there would be words and she wanted to make sure there was someone there who could help calm everyone down. Sadie had put in some time carefully planning the hymns and the scripture and she didn't want all of her work to be completely shot down," said Beatrice. "And Wyatt wasn't going to be exactly perfect to settle disputes—he was simply there to help coordinate the plans."

"You were there to say 'what a lovely suggestion!' to anything that Sadie came up with," said Meadow with a grin.

"Something like that. And Sadie was absolutely right. Hawkins became a lot more animated than he was when we were dropping the food off," said Beatrice.

"He would *have* to be more animated. Any *less* animated and he'd have been an inanimate object. A piece of furniture, or something," said Meadow. "What did he say about Sadie's suggestions?"

"Oh, he didn't like them. He thought that their father would have wanted more of a modern service," said Beatrice.

Meadow snorted. "As if! The man was as traditional as they come."

"Exactly. It was ridiculous. But then Hawkins kind of admitted that the service was more 'for the living' and *he* would be more comfortable with less of an 'ashes to ashes and dust to dust' type of service. Of course, I extolled Sadie's vision of the funeral, but when it came right down to it, I was determined to get out of that house at some point during the day. We started talking about compromises. That worked better," said Beatrice.

"Both traditional and modern," said Meadow, nodding. "And I bet fair-minded Wyatt liked a compromise solution, too. But what else? Did you find out anything else while you were there, or was it all about planning for the funeral?"

"Once everyone had left the room, Sadie did talk for a few minutes. Sadie seemed to know something and kept making references to 'being in the same house with a murderer' and that type of thing. But she said she didn't have any actual proof, so she didn't want to say whom she suspected," said Beatrice.

Noo-noo was now prancing in front of the window with little leaps, designed to get Beatrice's attention. The little dog grinned at them fetchingly through the window.

"Is Noo-noo putting on a show?" asked Meadow with delight.

"I think Noo-noo wants me to come in and feed her," said Beatrice wryly. "She's knocking herself out at this point, trying to get my attention. I'd better go." She hopped out of the car and then turned around and said, "Any news on Maisie yet? Still out roaming the woods somewhere?"

Meadow made a face. "I *hope* she's out roaming the woods. I'm a little worried. I hope she hasn't run into any trouble."

Beatrice said quickly, "I'll try to find some time to help Miss Sissy look again later. I also need to follow up on the little dog that's barking so much in the woods behind me."

"And we probably should check on June Bug and make sure that she's handling parenting all right," said Meadow, snapping her fingers.

"I meant to give her a call and with everything going on, I totally forgot about it."

"We've got a full plate, that's for sure," said Beatrice. Besides putting the finishing touches on her wedding, of course.

"Okay, see you at the guild meeting tomorrow! Eleven o'clock, my house!" sang out Meadow as she backed quickly out of Beatrice's driveway.

A few minutes later, there was a tap at the door and Beatrice frowned. Meadow *again*? She got up and looked out the front window. There she saw Wyatt's sister, Harper, smiling at her. Beatrice smiled back and reached to open the door. She put a hand to her hair to smooth it down. Harper was very kind and they got along well. It was just that Harper always managed to look immaculately put-together. She wore khaki Capri pants and a black, flowing top that set off her short, blonde bob. Her look was understated elegance. Beatrice's current look was 'needs a major overhaul.'

Harper gave her a hug and a rueful smile. "Sorry to just drop by like this. Ordinarily I'd call, but I happened to be driving past while you were on my mind." Noo-noo made a happy dance around Harper and she reached in her purse and produced a dog treat which he quickly devoured, grinning at Harper the whole time. Harper was nothing if not prepared.

"So good to see you!" said Beatrice. She glanced around. Thank goodness all the clutter had been shipped off to the Goodwill or else there wouldn't have been a place to sit down. "Won't you sit down?"

Harper said, "No, I couldn't do that to you. I'm sure you've got a million other things to be doing right now. I just feel terribly that I haven't been able to even take you out for dinner as your wedding date has gotten closer. Daniel and I meant to do that." She made a face and laughed. "Actually, I asked Wyatt to try and set something up a couple of weeks ago. He clearly forgot."

Beatrice smiled at her, but was thinking that she wasn't sure anything extra could *possibly* be fit into her schedule before the wedding day. She was having enough trouble even finding the time to spend with her groom. "Don't feel bad about it—it's been busy for all of us. I'm sure Wyatt just had so much on his mind that it totally slipped out of it."

"Oh, he's absentminded, all right! And he is, even when he's *not* about to be married. I have the feeling that the availability for a dinner is pretty much gone, isn't it?" asked Harper.

"Maybe coffee would be better, now that the wedding planning is in high gear," said Harper.

"How about coffee now? Here? I've got some wonderful Guatemalan coffee you might like. And lots of cream and sugar," said Beatrice.

"Are you sure you have time? On the spur of the moment?" asked Harper.

"Absolutely. And I could use a jolt of caffeine, considering what I've been doing," said Beatrice. As she made a pot of coffee and poured two cups, she told Harper about Caspian's death and the circumstances of it.

Harper frowned. "How awful. And how awful for you and Wyatt to have it happen during a pre-wedding event."

"It was very sad. I've been trying to help Ramsay ferret out some information."

Harper nodded. "I remember that you're very good at that."

"On top of it all, I spent early part of the afternoon frantically de-cluttering. Meadow helped me take a huge pile of things to Goodwill," said Beatrice.

Harper raised an eyebrow, "I'm assuming the cleanup was because of Wyatt's impending arrival?"

Beatrice laughed. "That's right. He's been so good about paring down his stuff so that we won't be crowded here. He was talking about getting rid of even *more* of his things and he's already given away a lot. I figured the least I could do was to meet him halfway."

"Well, it can be hard, can't it? After all, you've had a move recently, too. It's tough to get rid of things that you've had a long time," said Harper, setting down her coffee cup.

"I think I'm just more of a packrat than Wyatt is," said Beatrice with a sigh.

"Yes, but think of all the things you have to preserve! You were an *art museum curator*, Beatrice. And you've got quite a collection of art yourself." She paused. "Wyatt might, as well."

"Wyatt?" Beatrice knit her brows.

Harper said briskly, "Well, if he does, I'll let him introduce you to it. Now on to my present." She reached in her stylish black handbag and pulled out a beautifully-wrapped gift and handed it over to Beatrice. "Now, don't look at me like that. It's just something small that I thought might come in handy, that's all."

Beatrice opened the present and saw some beautifully monogrammed cream-colored stationery with her new initials: BCT.

"It's lovely, Harper, thanks," said Beatrice, giving Harper a warm smile. "And you're right—I already have lots of thank you notes to write."

Harper gave Noo-noo a quick rub and then stood up. "Good. I hoped you could use it. I'd better head out and leave you to rest for a few minutes. Although I have the feeling that might be easier said than done." She gave Beatrice a wry look. "You're not one to easily relax, especially with everything you have going on."

"That's true," said Beatrice, grinning. "Maybe I'll start on those thank you notes. Thanks for having coffee with me."

Beatrice did go over to Miss Sissy's later, to see if she needed some help finding the cat. But Miss Sissy wasn't there. Beatrice called her, since Miss Sissy was now a flip-phone cell phone user. A very grouchy Miss Sissy answered.

"Miss Sissy, can I meet you somewhere and help look for Maisie?" asked Beatrice politely.

The old woman sounded exasperated. "You've looked. Everybody's looked. Still gone."

"I know, but sometimes cats hide when they get out in unfamiliar territory. Maybe Maisie can even hear us calling her but isn't willing to leave her safe spot just yet. Lots of times cats come home all by themselves, even months later," said Beatrice, trying to put as optimistic a spin as possible on the situation.

Miss Sissy grunted, considering this.

"So why don't I join you for a little while and look?" asked Beatrice.

"Not now. Georgia is coming to look," said the old woman brusquely.

Beatrice was about to respond that a whole group of them had searched for Maisie the morning after she got out, but then she thought about it. Miss Sissy was probably right. If Maisie was being skittish, she was likely to be a lot *more* skittish if there was a group of three or more calling her.

"All right," said Beatrice. "Well, good luck. When you find her, could you give me a call or send me a text and let me know? I've been worried about her. And you."

Miss Sissy paused and then said in a gruff voice, "Me too. See you later." And she abruptly hung up.

Beatrice glanced at her watch. It was somehow already five-thirty in the evening. She listened and sure enough, she heard the dog barking frantically. She sighed and pulled on her shoes. Maybe the owners would be home at this time of the day, since they weren't home when she'd tried before.

She slogged through the woods for a while and then saw the golden retriever-collie mix still contained in the small, fenced back yard. The dog grinned in relief when he saw her, making little happy woofs in a voice that was hoarse from barking.

Beatrice walked around to the front of the house and sighed. She was going to have to try to approach this diplomatically. She imagined the owner might be defensive about neglecting the dog. But the fact was that the owner *was* neglecting the dog. The poor animal didn't deserve to be outside day and night. She knocked on the door.

A middle-aged woman, looking a bit suspicious and already defensive, answered the door. "Yes?" she asked sharply.

"Hi," said Beatrice with a smile. "I'm Beatrice Coleman—a neighbor of yours, actually. I live right through the woods, as a matter of fact."

The woman didn't return the smile or acknowledge that she knew if there was a house through the woods or not.

Beatrice took a deep breath and continued. She'd come this far. "I couldn't help but notice that your dog has been barking. Quite a lot, actually, and for the last couple of weeks."

The woman frowned at her. "Can't help that. He likes to bark."

Beatrice had more of an edge in her voice when she answered, "I can't imagine that he *likes* to bark. In fact, he seems positively hoarse from it. He seems to be distressed by the amount of time he's spending confined, by himself."

The woman put her hands on her hips and leaned forward, a bit aggressively. "Can't help that, either. Didn't want a dog to begin with. My dad had the dog and cancer took him a couple of weeks ago. Figured it'd be better for me to keep him outside than give him to the shelter. Don't reckon he'd last long there—they ain't got the room for no more animals, they said. They'd end up just putting him down."

Beatrice couldn't argue with that, but she pressed, "Sorry to hear about your father. But you don't know anyone else who could take the dog? He seems so friendly and it's really not fair to the animal to keep him in these circumstances."

Now the woman had a sly look on her face. "Nope. But *you* sure seem interested in the dog."

Beatrice said quickly, "Interested in his *well-being*."

"More than I am, probably," said the woman craftily.

"I already have a dog," said Beatrice, growing alarmed.

"He gets along good with other dogs. Least, that's what my dad said," said the woman. She patted her pocket and pulled out a pack of cigarettes.

"Look, I'm planning a wedding here. Among other things," said Beatrice in a rush.

"Be a pity if a fine animal like that ends up at the shelter," said the woman dourly.

Beatrice closed her eyes for a moment and sighed. This was bad timing. She didn't need a dog. But she seemed to be better-positioned to find a good home for the dog than this woman.

"I'll take him off your hands," said Beatrice between gritted teeth.

"I'll get him on a leash for you," said the woman with alacrity. She disappeared into the small house, reappearing moments later with the dog. The dog erupted into wiggles when spotting Beatrice. He threw himself on his back for a tummy rub.

Beatrice bent to rub him. As she was standing back up, the woman was already closing the door without as much as a goodbye to the dog.

"Wait a minute!" called Beatrice. "What's his name?"

"Scooter," she said briefly. "And he's had all his shots and is fixed." With that, she closed the door firmly behind her.

Noo-noo looked skeptically at Scooter as Beatrice walked through the front door of the cottage.

"It's okay, Noo-noo," she murmured to him. "This is just temporary." But as she said it, she crossed her fingers. She knew that most of her friends already had dogs or cats and might not need another pet.

Scooter seemed happy to see the corgi and happily approached Noo-noo with his tail up and wagging. His tongue lolled out and he bowed in front of the little dog to show he was ready to play. Noo-noo joined in and soon the two dogs were chasing each other.

With the dogs getting along well, the rest of the day, Beatrice attempted to work on her quilt in time for the guild meeting the next day. She wanted at least to be able to report *some* progress on it when everyone else would likely be showing off finished quilts and explaining their new projects or ideas that they had.

Before she knew it, it was time to turn in. Wyatt called her on the phone to say goodnight, which had become their habit. She always felt more relaxed when he called her up and felt like she was putting the day behind her. Beatrice told him about Harper's visit and then about the cleaning out she'd done earlier.

"By the way, do you know anyone who needs a dog?" she asked wryly.

Wyatt said, "Not offhand—why? Noo-noo isn't getting on your nerves, is she?" he asked in a teasing voice.

"Oh Noo-noo is perfectly behaved, as usual. But I accidentally adopted that barking dog in the house behind me. Remember my telling you about it?" asked Beatrice.

"This is the same barking dog that's been keeping you up at night? And waking you up in the morning?" asked Wyatt.

"That's right. Although he hasn't made a single peep since he's been here. I think he was just frantically trying to make human contact. The woman who owned him didn't want him and she was keeping him outside day and night. Scooter must have been so lonely."

"The dog's name is Scooter?" asked Wyatt.

"Yes, and I'm actively searching for a new owner," said Beatrice with a sigh. "Having another dog is the last thing I need right now."

"I'll check around," said Wyatt.

"I will, too," said Beatrice. "Thanks Wyatt. Sleep tight."

That night, she had the first really good night's sleep for weeks. She'd made a bed for Scooter on some towels near Noo-noo's bed, but the next morning she found the dog lying quietly next to her bedside, keeping a watchful eye on her as she slept. She had her breakfast, took both dogs for a quick walk, and got ready for the guild meeting. She put on some black cropped pants and a white button-down shirt, smeared on a dab of pink lipstick, made a face at herself in the mirror, and replaced it with red lipstick. She looked too washed out without it.

Noo-noo needed a little more love and reassurance before Beatrice left, so she stooped to rub the corgi's tummy for a few minutes. Then Noo-noo clambered into her lap to lick her face. Beatrice discovered that in the process, she'd become covered with corgi fur—and that somehow Noo-noo had cleverly managed to get her white fur on Beatrice's black pants and her sable/red fur on Beatrice's white top. Scooter stood grinning at them. She glanced at her watch. No time to change now. She brushed herself off as quickly as she could and then hurried out to her car.

Beatrice parked outside the beautiful old barn where Meadow lived, and frowned. She must be even later than she'd thought. Everyone was already here—she must be the last person to arrive, judging from the cars and from Savannah's and Georgia's bikes here. Maybe Beatrice had gotten the time wrong. Even Miss Sissy's dilapidated Lincoln was there. Beatrice wondered if Miss Sissy had found Maisie or if maybe she'd decided to come to the guild meeting to recruit shifts of searchers. She made a mental note to help scour the woods for the missing cat later. Her life seemed to be rapidly taken over by animals recently.

Still brushing off the errant dog fur, Beatrice hurried into Meadow's house.

"Surprise!" came a crescendo of a yell and Beatrice was greeted with the sight of the entire guild, some of whom hadn't come to the last couple of meetings, beaming at her.

Chapter Ten

Balloons in every color were tied on every available chair and table leg (likely to keep the balloons from flying up to the steep ceiling of the barn). There was a table of gifts off to the side, all in bright wrapping paper. And everyone seemed to be there, including her too-busy, misty-eyed daughter, Piper. Even Miss Sissy was there, probably pulled out of searching the woods, smiling at her. Beatrice felt herself tear up and blinked hard to fight the uncharacteristic tears.

Meadow bounced over to her. She carried a plate that was completely covered with food. Beatrice spotted stuffed mushrooms, deviled eggs, sausage bites, brie with pepper jelly, and cheese straws. Beatrice laughed shakily, "And now, suddenly, I'm starving. And trying not to cry at the same time. How can I thank y'all? What a lovely surprise!"

Meadow said, now dabbing tears herself, "We knew you wouldn't let us give you a shower if you knew about it. So we had to give one in secret!"

Savannah and Georgia both gave her hugs, Georgia very effusively and Savannah with her usual restraint (but with a warm smile and an unusual twinkle in her eye). Georgia said, "We wanted to do something and figured this was the only way to do it!"

Savannah said, "I'm glad you didn't lug a quilt here! I was worried that you were going expect us to be doing some quilting."

Beatrice laughed. "I actually only needed quilt inspiration today. But I bet I can get that at my shower, too. I can't thank y'all enough." She saw Piper grinning at her, near the refreshments table. "And you're here, too! You didn't give me any hints at all that this was in the works."

Piper said, "I don't think you've ever really been truly *surprised* by a party before. I wanted to see if we could pull it off! I remember a group of us tried to surprise you when you turned fifty, but you saw right through it. You're way too good at figuring out mysteries." Then she blushed a little and pinched her mouth shut, remembering that Sadie and Della, who had a mystery of their own, were standing close nearby.

But before Beatrice could say anything to them, Meadow engulfed her in another hug. "Go ahead and sit down and start eating so that the rest of us can eat!" she demanded, still wiping a stray tear or two away as she gently pushed Beatrice toward a chair. "And so we can move on to the cake! It looks like one of June Bug's best."

June Bug smiled shyly. Most of the women headed in the direction of the kitchen to help themselves to a plate.

Beatrice sat and was soon joined by Savannah, who perched stiffly in a wooden armchair.

"I don't think I've ever been so surprised in my life," said Beatrice. "I was sure it was going to be a guild meeting. It's a good thing that I didn't bring a bunch of quilting things with me."

Savannah said in a pleased voice, "I've never been part of a surprise party before. It's surprisingly difficult to execute. You have to be prepared to lie about the reason for the party, which keeps you on your toes."

"Well, I was surprised enough to invite two guests to our meeting," said Beatrice with a laugh. "So you and everyone else did a good job. I suppose Meadow must have mentioned to them that it wasn't a *real* guild meeting? At least, I hope she did!"

Savannah gave a quick nod. "She did at that. Told them if they wanted to experience a *real* guild meeting, they should come to the next one." Savannah shifted uncomfortably. "This isn't *officially* a guild meeting, of course. Although we set it up as one. We're definitely not following our guild bylaws."

This seemed to trouble Savannah a bit. Savannah was always a stickler for the rules.

"Sometimes it's good to deviate from the regular guild program to do something fun," said Savannah's sister, Georgia, joining them with a smile.

Savannah said quickly, "Although, if you *wanted* it to be more of a guild meeting, Beatrice, I could discuss quilting whilst others are filling their plates. That way, we might cover all the bases."

Georgia winked at Beatrice surreptitiously. "Savannah does like to go by the book."

Beatrice decided it might be a good idea to soothe Savannah a bit. "Sure. Tell me what you're working on now." She took a big bite of deviled eggs. She decided that she'd have to ask Meadow what she put in them to make them so good.

Georgia said, "Oh, Beatrice will never guess what you're working on now, Savannah."

"A geometric pattern?" asked Beatrice innocently.

"Yes, yes, but you don't know what *type* of geometric pattern. I chose something quite different this time."

Georgia winked again at Beatrice.

Savannah continued with dignity, "It's a Tahoe pattern with very cheerful colors. Lots of reds and greens."

"And a lot of diagonals!" said Georgia.

"That's what makes it challenging," said Savannah. "And fun. It's made with a ton of fat quarters ... I'm sure Posy was happy to see me shopping as much as I was."

Georgia laughed. "Savannah, I'm seriously hoping that this conversation shifts to wedding planning, even if it *is* supposed to be a guild meeting. I'm going to get some of Meadow's delicious food—be right back."

Savannah waited until Georgia had gotten out of earshot and then glanced swiftly around them. Everyone else was still loading their plates. Savannah leaned closer to Beatrice and said conspiratorially, "You know what? I *am* making something that's not geometric."

Beatrice exclaimed, "Another quilt at the same time? Now I'm really feeling like a slacker."

Savannah said, "It's a special quilt. You know—a special project. It's all hearts and flowers."

"For Georgia and Tony?" said Beatrice, smiling. "Oh, Savannah. She'll love it."

Savannah turned pink and looked pleased. "I hope so," she said modestly. Then she frowned. "It's not my usual type of project at all, you know. I'm used to all the straight lines and perfect angles. This quilt is a lot trickier than I thought it would be, although it's coming along."

"How has everything else been going for you, Savannah?" asked Beatrice. "How is Smoke?"

Smoke was Savannah's young cat. He was absolutely adorable, especially when Georgia made outfits for him. And he was the apple of Savannah's eye. Beatrice had reflected before that it was really a blessing that Savannah had Smoke to dote on, especially since Georgia had been so preoccupied with Tony: first with dating him, then with their engagement.

Savannah said, "Smoke is doing all right, but I honestly think he's sad about Maisie being missing. You know that he and Maisie were friends and that I'd even bring Smoke over to visit Maisie at the shop or at Miss Sissy's house. You wouldn't think cats would be that social, but these two are. Now we haven't visited Maisie for a while and Smoke seems really sad."

Beatrice nodded. "I'm hoping Maisie turns up soon. Maybe it won't be long now that she ends up back with Miss Sissy."

"I hope so." She glanced at the refreshments and then said with a bit of alarm, "I'd better hurry over there before all the food is gone! Meadow's food goes too fast."

"Especially with Miss Sissy eating," noted Beatrice wryly.

Savannah's eyes grew wide. "Indeed!" She rushed to the kitchen, passing Miss Sissy and her tremendous plate of food on the way.

As Miss Sissy plopped down next to Beatrice, Beatrice saw that her plate was laden with foods of all kinds. And Beatrice had no doubt that the old woman would go back for both second and third helpings, if there was any food left. She wondered if Miss Sissy had eaten regular meals at all since Maisie had disappeared.

"Do you have any updates on Maisie, Miss Sissy?" asked Beatrice.

Miss Sissy looked down at her food and her lip trembled just a bit. She shook her head.

Beatrice said in a rush, "But everyone in Dappled Hills is looking for her. I'm sure she'll be found soon."

Someone cleared their throat behind them and they turned to see little June Bug standing there. She looked earnestly at Miss Sissy, "I'm sure I saw Maisie today on the way over here."

Miss Sissy's eyes grew wide, "Where?" she gasped.

"In the woods between Beatrice's house and Meadow's. It looked just like Maisie. I stopped the car and hopped out and called her, but she ran away," said June Bug looking sorrowful.

Miss Sissy said, "But she was okay?"

"She looked great. She just didn't want to come to me," said June Bug.

For a moment Miss Sissy looked as if she were about to leap up, leave the shower, and head off into the woods again. But then she hesitated, looking at her plate of food.

Beatrice said quickly, "Miss Sissy, Maisie can wait. She'll probably have moved on by the time we get there. Besides, I'm wondering how often you're eating meals. Why don't you finish eating, take a break, and then we can look some more?"

Miss Sissy nodded slowly and then attacked her plate of food with vigor.

June Bug cleared her throat and shyly said, "Everyone? I want to introduce you to my niece, Katy."

Now Beatrice saw that a small girl was hovering behind June Bug. She was very thin, had straight brown hair, and serious blue eyes. She gave a tentative smile as everyone greeted her.

Meadow said, "Katy, I bet I know what might be fun for you. I still have some of Ash's toys here. How about if you come over to the other side of the kitchen and I'll set up a play area for you? It might be more fun than listening to a bunch of old women gossip."

Katy hesitated, and then nodded slightly, eyes trained on the floor. Meadow reached out a hand to Katy and she took it, walking away to get the toys.

Beatrice asked June Bug in a low voice, "How is everything going with Katy?"

June Bug's round face looked worried. "Oh Beatrice, I don't know. She doesn't ever say a word. She's so quiet and serious."

Katy sounded, actually, quite a bit like June Bug, herself.

Beatrice said, "I'm sure she'll be fine. She just has a lot to adjust to … especially the loss of her mom. It may just take her a while."

June Bug nodded, but the anxiety remained in her eyes as she watched Katy carefully building block towers in a corner of Meadow's kitchen. Then Piper came over to talk with June Bug about Katy's adjustment to school and Beatrice visited with Posy.

A few minutes later, Piper teasingly said to Meadow, "Your food is just too good. You're going to have to teach me how to cook some of Ash's favorite meals. Otherwise, after the wedding, he'll be over *here* all the time to be fed instead of at our house!"

Meadow waved her away, "Oh, I'm sure your mother has taught you a lot about cooking."

Beatrice choked a bit on her deviled eggs.

Piper said diplomatically, "Well, Mama has always been so busy. We ate out a lot, didn't we?"

Beatrice nodded, grateful for the life buoy. Beatrice had indeed been busy after her husband passed away. But it probably would have been good to teach Piper how to cook. If, that is, she'd figured it out a bit better, herself.

Meadow grinned over at Sadie and Della. "We're so glad that you two came to join us today! Although it's a most-unusual guild meeting for us. Will y'all come back again when we have a real meeting? We have a lot of fun."

Sadie said to Meadow, "That's a deal. Will it be next month?"

"No, we won't wait that long, especially since this was a faux meeting just to lure Beatrice here." Her eyes opened wide. "Wouldn't it have been awful if Beatrice had had some kind of conflict or forgotten to come? I'd have had to run over to her cottage and kidnap her."

"That wouldn't be the first time that happened," said Beatrice dryly.

Meadow and Sadie started talking about the nuts-and-bolts of the guild and the kinds of things they'd done lately: charity quilt drives, mystery quilts, fabric swaps, and show-and-tells. Della smiled, but didn't seem to be engaging in the conversation much.

Beatrice said to Della, "Thanks for coming—that's really sweet of you, considering that you've already helped host something for me earlier."

Della perked up a bit at the compliment. "Oh, I didn't mind. Anything to get out of the house at this point. It's pretty grim there."

"I can imagine," said Beatrice. "At least you've got the funeral plans set, it sounds like. And I hope you'll come out to the next, real guild meeting. We do have a lot of fun, and I get a lot of inspiration from the other women."

Della nodded, looking around the room. "They've all been quilting for a while?"

"Some of them, like Miss Sissy, their whole lives," said Beatrice, nodding. "But I know you're just starting out with the craft."

Della seized on this. "Exactly. I'm not even sure if it's something I want to spend a *lot* of time doing. I might be more interested in doing lots of different crafts instead of focusing on just one. And I wouldn't want to end up having to be an officer in a guild or something like that. I don't think I'd have enough time."

Beatrice nodded slowly. "I can understand that. You're just trying different crafts out and trying to find a good fit. But do come to a guild meeting—I think it'll give you a good overview of what being involved in the quilting community can be."

She smiled at Della and Della smiled back. If Della only knew how lucky it was that *Beatrice* had been the one to recruit her and not the heavy-handed Meadow.

Meadow was now busy commandeering the bridal shower. She clapped her hands. "Ladies? There seems to be a little food left over, if anyone wants seconds."

Miss Sissy immediately got up and started heading to the kitchen.

"And now it's time for presents! My favorite part!" said Meadow, eyes gleaming.

Beatrice felt herself blushing a bit. "You're all too kind. You really didn't have to. At my age, I'm not exactly going from my parents' home to my new husband's. I have a good bit of stuff."

Meadow said, "Pooh! A no-gift shower is no fun at all. And this shower is all about fun. Starting off with the fact that it was a surprise. How many surprise showers have you been to?" she demanded.

Beatrice laughed. "I've never, ever been to a surprise shower. All right, you've convinced me. On to the gifts!"

Chapter Eleven

Beatrice opened Piper's gift first. She smiled and gave her daughter a big hug when she saw a gift certificate to her and Wyatt's favorite restaurant in downtown Dappled Hills.

"I wanted to give you an excuse to go out for a few nights on the town," said Piper, teasingly. "I know how you both try to save money, but sometimes it's just important to get out."

Everyone oohed and ahhed and laughed when Beatrice opened Georgia's present. It was a white satiny bandana that had 'happily ever after' and the date of the wedding stitched on it with a cream-colored cotton flower on it.

The ever-practical Savannah had given her an account ledger. She said eagerly to Beatrice, "I thought combining the accounts of two different households might be tricky. I monogrammed the cover for you, myself," she added, proudly.

Beatrice gave her a hug, feeling her eyes prickle with tears—not so much at the gift itself but how much time and thought her friend had put into purchasing something for her.

Posy held out her gift to Beatrice. It was in a large box and wrapped beautifully in patches of various gift wraps to give it a quilting flavor. "Hope you'll enjoy it," she said with a twinkle in her eye. "Here—be a bit careful ... it's a little fragile."

Beatrice was *extremely* careful at that point, because just hearing that something was fragile was enough to turn her completely into butterfingers. She carefully unwrapped the gift and pulled back the tissue paper inside to reveal a handmade birdfeeder: a replica of Dappled Hills Presbyterian Church where Wyatt preached. Even the ivy climbing up the sides of the church and the steeple were represented. Beatrice gasped. "It's gorgeous, Posy! Did *you* make this?"

Posy's eyes crinkled and she gave her gentle laugh. "Oh, no. No, I'm no good at all with woodworking or models or anything. Cork made this."

"*Cork* did? I had no idea he could make something like this," said Beatrice.

"Me either!" Meadow put her hands on her hips. "How secretive of him!"

Posy smiled. "He'll be so pleased you like it, Beatrice. I think he's kept his talent a secret because he's not only a little insecure about it, but he also wants to make things for himself and not so much for others."

Meadow sighed. "So he won't be taking orders, then?"

"If he does, you'll be the first to know," said Posy, grinning.

Beatrice said, "It's so pretty that I almost don't want to put it outside for the birds!"

"Oh no, it's designed for the birds and for being outdoors. He did something to weatherproof it," said Posy.

Beatrice gave Posy a hug. And then gave her another one. "For Cork," she said.

Meadow's gift was next. Beatrice unwrapped it to find a treasure trove of fabrics, notions she'd never even seen before, and patterns. Beatrice grinned at her. "Wyatt will love these."

Meadow laughed and said, "Actually, you're *right*. 'Happy wife, happy life.'"

Sadie held out and envelope and said with a smile, "From Della and me."

Beatrice flushed. "Oh, you didn't have to do that."

"I know. We *wanted* to."

Inside the envelope was a gift card for a manicure and pedicure in nearby Lenoir.

Della said with her eyes partially closed and a smile on her face, "It's the best mani-pedi *ever*."

Sadie added, "We thought you might need something relaxing with all the stress of a wedding going on."

Beatrice thanked them and then saw what looked like a banker's box with a lid on it.

"From Miss Sissy," said Meadow.

Beatrice approached the box a little cautiously. With Miss Sissy, you never really knew what you were going to get.

Inside was a lovely old quilt. It wasn't just an 'old' quilt. It was vintage, an heirloom. And, for a moment, Beatrice's art curator background took over as she studied it. It was an appliqued Tree of Life quilt and the stitching was impeccable. The quilt was in wonderful shape and the reds and blues of the bird perching in the branches of the tree were nearly as bright as they must have been one hundred years earlier.

"It's beautiful," said Beatrice reverently.

Miss Sissy smiled at her, her blue eyes bright. "Was Mother's. She made it," she said gruffly.

"She was an amazing quilter," said Beatrice gently. "Although I never thought otherwise—after all, her daughter is such an amazing quilter." She hesitated. "Are you sure you want me to have this? It's one of your heirlooms."

Miss Sissy glared at her. "Of course! Needs to be enjoyed. Too many quilts at home."

Beatrice ran her hand softly over the needlework of the applique. "We'll take good care of it, Miss Sissy. This means a lot to us. Thank you."

The last gift was from a round-eyed June Bug who blushed as Beatrice reached for her gift.

"I have a hard time deciding on gifts," said the little woman, shifting from one foot to the other.

Beatrice opened the little box to find an exquisitely made dainty handkerchief with tiny blue flowers.

"June Bug! This is beautiful," said Beatrice.

June Bug's eyes shone as she looked shyly at Beatrice. "Do you think so? Mother made it a long time ago."

Meadow exclaimed, "Something old! And something blue, too—the little flowers!"

Beatrice said quickly, "May I give it back to you after the wedding? You may want to give it to Katy one day. I remember that you said before that you don't have many of your mother's things left anymore. That way, this will also be something *borrowed*, too."

"Three in one!" said Savannah. The sheer efficiency of it delighted her.

Beatrice was afraid that she would offend June Bug by returning her precious gift later, but if anything, the little woman looked even more pleased. "Three in one," she repeated with a happy smile.

The bridal shower was wrapping up and everyone had made their goodbyes but Beatrice.

Beatrice remembered something and quickly called out, "By the way, does anyone need a dog?" She laughed. "Or maybe I should ask if anyone *wants* a dog. I happen to know a very friendly, cute one who is looking for a home!"

Everyone laughed, shaking their heads. Beatrice sighed. She really hoped she wasn't going to end up being the long-term solution for Scooter.

"Did you take that dog on?" asked Meadow. "The one that's been driving you crazy with all his racket?"

"I sure did," said Beatrice. "But he's quiet as can be when he's with people. It's just being confined outside day in and day out that made him bark."

Meadow said, "I'll ask around a little. Maybe I can find someone."

Beatrice hugged her quilting friends as they left. Meadow looked at her suspiciously as Beatrice lingered. "You are *not* allowed to help clean up! This was a party for *you*."

Beatrice held up her hands and laughed. "I wouldn't dream of it. I just wanted to thank you again for putting this together."

Meadow put a plate in the dishwasher. "Wasn't it a great shower? And everyone came! Having your shower take the place of a guild meeting was a stroke of brilliance, I must say. There's no way you'd have let me host one, otherwise. Now, let me help you put your presents in your car for you."

Beatrice shook her head. "No need. Savannah and Georgia already did. Everyone's kept me completely lazy today."

"Because it's your special day!" retorted Meadow. "Now all you need to do is to go back home, pour yourself a glass of wine, and read your book out in your hammock." She snapped her fingers. "Which reminds me! Ramsay gave me another book for you to read. Oh, he'd have really rolled his eyes if I'd forgotten. He insisted that you needed something to read now, even through all the chaos you've got going on."

Beatrice wasn't at all sure that she needed a book to read right now. There was, as Meadow pointed out, the wedding-related chaos. There was also the fact that she was trying to help solve Caspian's murder. She was part of a search team for a missing cat and the hopefully temporary owner of a second dog. And, add the fact that she was trying to squeeze some quilting in, her life was pretty busy.

"I hope it's not another *Moby Dick*," said Beatrice with a sigh.

Meadow strategically stuffed another couple of glasses into the dishwasher and started it up. "I agree. The very idea of saddling a bride-to-be with *Moby Dick*! All those harpoons and nets and fish and whatnot. Ramsay must have lost what was left of his mind. *Surely* this must be a better choice." She grunted. "Although he's not been at all perceptive these days. It must be the murder investigation. Watch him have chosen a book by Steinbeck or Hemingway or something equally grim for you to read."

"Either one of those would be an improvement on Melville. At least for right now," said Beatrice.

Meadow said, "I'll run get it. Oh, and let Boris out. The poor guy. I know he must have been dying to join the party, but I thought he might be a bit distracting."

She disappeared into the master bedroom, off the main room of the barn. Beatrice shuddered. She could only imagine what a bridal shower with Boris would have been like. He'd have been competing with Miss Sissy to see how much food he could eat. He'd have leapt on every guest as they came in. There'd have been big puddles of drool on all the gifts. He was a sweet dog, and Beatrice had come to appreciate his offbeat personality, but he was nowhere near as well-behaved as her Noo-noo. Nor, she suspected, nearly as bright. And she had the feeling that Scooter also far outshone Boris in intellectual capacity and behavior, too.

Boris came bounding out, head swinging around as if looking for any crumbs that might have made their way to the floor. When he spotted Beatrice, his eyes lit up and he came careening over to her, sliding on the hardwood floor until he crashed into her. Luckily, Beatrice had had the good sense to drop into a chair before the impact so she wasn't bowled completely over.

Meadow beamed at the tremendous dog. "What a sweet boy. He's so happy to see you!"

"I can't believe you managed to contain him with all the sights and smells of the party," said Beatrice, gingerly petting Boris as he leaned his head on her knees, his tongue lolling out.

Meadow said, "Oh, it was a piece of cake. I turned on the bathroom fan *and* the white noise sound machine that we had. Then I turned on the TV to this ambient music station that we have. On top of *that*, I gave him his favorite Kong and stuffed it with treats and peanut butter. He sort of had his own party."

Beatrice said, "Glad it worked. What's the verdict on the book?"

Meadow grinned at her. "Oh, I think you're going to like it." She held out the book to her.

Beatrice smiled. "Yes. Yes, this might be the perfect book for right now."

And she drove back home with *The Wind in the Willows* sitting in the passenger seat next to her.

Later in the day, Beatrice realized that she'd forgotten to get stamps the last time she'd run errands. And now that she had new stationery from Harper, she certainly needed to have stamps worthy of them.

She was just walking into the post office when she saw Wyatt's best friend, James, walking out. He grinned at her in his friendly way. In fact, Beatrice thought, most of the time she saw James, he had a smile on his face. He was also a lot more casually dressed than she usually saw him. James had grown up with Wyatt in Dappled Hills, but then had moved away to go to school, med school, and to practice medicine. He'd moved back five years ago to practice medicine in his hometown. Now he was Wyatt's best man.

"You must have the day off," said Beatrice, giving him a smile. "Unless it's casual day at the doctor's office."

"Oh, I'd love to be able to get away with *that*," said James, grinning. "No, if I showed up in shorts and a golf shirt, I'd scare off my patients. I've got the day off and am about to go fishing. The fish bite more at the beginning and end of the day."

Beatrice said, "You've got to be ready for a break. From what I've seen, your doctor's office is swamped all the time. It's a tiny town, but I guess when there are only a couple of doctor's offices, they stay busy."

"True, although I'm not as busy as Wyatt is. Ministers don't really ever have a day off, do they? Of course, I never thought he was going to be a minister, growing up." James took a second to greet someone walking into the post office.

Beatrice paused and then asked, "You didn't? What did you think he was going to be?"

"Oh, an artist. For sure! Although I'm sure his parents tried to talk him out of it. Artists aren't particularly well-known for being able to make a living," said James.

"An *artist*?" Beatrice stared at him.

"Sure! He was always sketching or painting or taking pictures. It's what he loved to do," said James.

"I had no idea," said Beatrice slowly. The idea that she didn't know something important about Wyatt was a surprise to her. They'd had so many long conversations together.

"Well, he's probably too busy now with the church to do much of anything in his spare time. But you should ask him about it." James glanced at his watch and grinned. "All right, I'd better head on out. Those fish are waiting for me."

Beatrice gave him an absent smile as he left and she walked into the post office. She tried to think of any paintings or art in Wyatt's small house that might have been artwork of his, but she couldn't think of anything. Surely he hadn't gotten rid of some of his work while trying to get ready to move to Beatrice's house?

She bought her stamps and got back into the car. On the way back, she decided to stop by the church and see Wyatt. She wanted to ask him about his old hobby and find out if he was still creating. After all, both Harper and James had alluded to his art. It must have been important to him.

Wyatt was just walking out of the church when her car pulled into the parking lot. He looked tired, but as soon as he saw Beatrice, he smiled.

"This is a nice surprise," he said.

"It looks like you've had a long day," said Beatrice.

"Oh, it's been setting the church budget today. That's always a lot more draining than my usual work. And I probably need to do some packing when I get back to the house—maybe some of the nicer china and crystal that I won't be using until after the wedding," said Wyatt.

"I'll help you," said Beatrice. "I hope you've got lots of newspaper to wrap them in."

When they arrived at Wyatt's house, Beatrice saw that newspaper wasn't a problem. There was a large stack of it, along with flattened boxes and rolls of packing tape. It was all very organized-looking.

They chatted about their days for a few minutes while they carefully wrapped the china and crystal. Beatrice finally couldn't wait any longer to ask Wyatt.

"I ran into James today at the post office," she said slowly.

Wyatt raised his eyebrows. "Was he taking a lunch break?"

"No, he had the day off and was about to go fishing. But he did mention something that I found interesting. Actually, Harper had sort of hinted at the same thing when I talked to her earlier," said Beatrice.

"Now you've *really* whetted my interest," said Wyatt in a teasing voice.

"James mentioned that he'd always thought, growing up, that you were going to be an artist," said Beatrice, watching Wyatt closely.

A hint of a red blush rose from Wyatt's neck. He quickly shook his head and said, "That was just an old childhood dream. You know. When all kids wanted to be astronauts or vets or archeologists or something."

"I don't think that being an artist is the same sort of dream as being an astronaut," said Beatrice. When he didn't immediately answer, she said, "You must have been really good."

Wyatt snorted and Beatrice followed up quickly with: "Or at least must have enjoyed it a lot."

"I did, actually. I really enjoyed it—especially the sketches. It was just a very calming activity to sit outside and sketch," said Wyatt. He sounded a little cautious.

Clearly, Wyatt was insecure about his artwork. Beatrice said, "I'd really love to see some of it."

"I'm not even sure that I can put my hands on it," said Wyatt. "After all, I've been packing for the last couple of weeks. And besides, it's not very good."

Beatrice raised her eyebrows. "Are you sure that you're the best judge of that? Most artists don't get enough distance from their work to be able to assess whether it's good or not."

Wyatt smiled at her. "I'd hardly call myself an artist."

"An artist is someone who creates art," said Beatrice briskly. "There's nothing more to it than that. It's not some sort of mystical club."

"I think that my problem is that you're a very *good* evaluator of art. You were an art museum curator, after all. It's not like passing art by someone who doesn't know what they're doing," said Wyatt. "And I think your interest in my art probably stems from the fact that you love me." His voice was light, but there was a cloud of concern in his eyes.

Beatrice recognized the concern. Artists were frequently insecure about their work. Sharing your art with someone was a huge step.

"Of *course* it stems from the fact I love you!" she said in an impatient voice. "But that's only part of it. Another part is that I'm genuinely curious. I'm a curious person, if you haven't noticed. Why else would I be investigating murders in my spare time?"

Wyatt's smile was broader now and a bit more confident, although his eyes still had that hint of uncertainty. "I'll try to pull some of the paintings out while I'm packing."

"Great! I'll find some room on my walls to display it." At the somewhat panicked expression on Wyatt's face, Beatrice added quickly, "That is, only if you want to. Although I'd love to."

"Wait until you see it first," protested Wyatt. "And no matter how good it might be, there is no way it can compete with the masterpieces you have hanging up on your walls."

Beatrice started to protest and then stopped herself. She *had* collected a lot of art through the years and some of it was quite good. It would be easy to be intimidated as an artist by sharing a wall with some really excellent pieces.

"Hanging anything up is totally up to you," she said, reaching out to give him a hug. "Just remember that I'm always proud of you, no matter what."

He held on to her tightly before tilting back to look at her with his eyes full of love.

Chapter Twelve

The next morning, Meadow called her. It was bright and early—early enough that Beatrice wasn't even dressed yet.

"I'm trying to reach Sadie and I can't get her on the phone," fussed Meadow.

Beatrice sighed. "Meadow, she might not even be awake yet. It's pretty early in the day. Why not just try again later?"

"But she told me that she was an early riser. I've decided to have the *real* guild meeting the day after Caspian's funeral. I thought it would be a nice distraction after a hard day," said Meadow.

"When *is* Caspian's funeral?" asked Beatrice.

"I've no idea! And Ramsay is no help at all. He says that the police are finished with the autopsy and have released Caspian to the care of a funeral home. But I can't get any information one way or the other. And the funeral home won't comment because they say it's in the family's hands." Meadow's voice was frustrated. "I was trying to confirm the time and date of the service to make sure I can host the guild meeting the following day."

Beatrice said, "Well, if she isn't sleeping, I'm sure she has her hands full. Maybe she's trying to go through her father's things, or settle business, or even work out the final details of the service. Maybe she's even trying to catch up on her sleep, for heaven's sake. Just give her a couple of hours and try again. It's hardly an emergency—the service is most likely going to be in the next couple of days."

It was a couple of hours later when Meadow showed up at her door. By this point, Beatrice had gotten dressed, had a leisurely breakfast, called Wyatt to check in on his day and update him on the quilting bridal shower, and had gone into the backyard with Noo-noo and Scooter and *The Wind in the Willows*. This explained why she had no idea that there was an agitated Meadow at her front door.

Beatrice was just laughing at Toad's antics when a face popped up over her fence. Noo-noo, startled, started barking in earnest.

"It's okay, Noo-noo," said Beatrice soothingly. "It's just Meadow."

Meadow, however, looked as though nothing was all right. "Something's happened," she gasped. "Trying to catch my breath."

Beatrice got out of the hammock and slid open the latch on her back gate to allow Meadow in. "What on earth? Did you *run* all the way down here?"

"No, no. The car's out front. But still—ran around the back." Meadow plopped down in a patio chair and Beatrice hurried off to get her a lemonade.

"Whatever it is can wait until you have a drink," called Beatrice behind her as she headed for the kitchen. Noo-noo leaned against Meadow, peering up anxiously at her.

When Beatrice returned, Meadow gratefully took the glass and drained it quickly. "Ramsay was called out to the Nelms estate again a few minutes ago. Hawkins found her. Oh, isn't it awful? It won't do Hawkins any good, and we know what terrible shape he was in before!"

Beatrice took a deep breath in an attempt to rein in her rapidly departing patience. "Meadow, slow down. I don't have the slightest clue what you're talking about. Hawkins found *who*?"

"Sadie," said Meadow miserably. "Sadie is dead. Oh, I knew something was wrong. I had a bad feeling about it when I couldn't reach her this morning. Hawkins was taking a walk around the estate this morning with Barkis and he came across her body. And that's all I know!"

Beatrice took the empty glass away from her since Meadow was so agitated that Beatrice had visions of the glass flying across the patio.

Meadow said, "We should go over there. Right now."

"I don't know if that's a wise thing to do, Meadow. We'll get in Ramsay's way. He'll be wanting to bring in the state police and check for clues in the house and on the grounds. Plus, he'll need to interview the family once again," said Beatrice.

Meadow insisted, "Which is exactly why we need to be there! We need to find out what's going on over there. Give Wyatt a call and accompany him there to comfort the family. Maybe you can get information from them surreptitiously."

"What will *your* excuse be for going over there?" asked Beatrice wryly.

"Oh, to bring comfort, myself! In the form of food," said Meadow.

Beatrice said, "I know you're very talented in the kitchen, but surely even *you* weren't able to whip up a family-sized bereavement meal in the last ten minutes."

"No, which is why we need to stop at June Bug's bakery to pick up goodies on the way," said Meadow. She frowned. "Actually, to save time, I'll call June Bug and place an order so she can be working on pulling it together. If you can call Wyatt?"

And Meadow hurried off, phone in hand, into Beatrice's cottage.

They picked up Wyatt first. He was at the church in his office when he got the call. He listened calmly to Beatrice, making concerned sounds as she told him what little she knew. They drove to June Bug's shop while Wyatt called Malcolm and told him they were on their way over.

June Bug was flushed when they arrived at the bakery.

"I think I've got it all together," the little woman said breathlessly as she stuffed everything into bags. "There are quiches, pecan sticky buns, croissants, and muffins."

"Carbohydrates will absorb the shock," said Meadow, sounding knowledgeable. She paid June Bug, and Wyatt picked up the two, large paper grocery bags.

June Bug said in her quiet voice to Beatrice, "Um ... about your dog. Could I talk to you about it later?"

Beatrice blinked in surprise and then said quickly, "Definitely! If you're thinking about a dog for Katy, this one might be a good fit. Why don't you come by *without* Katy after work today? Then, if you like Scooter, you could bring Katy the next time."

June Bug smiled and nodded, bustling back into her kitchen with a wave.

Minutes later, Meadow pulled up in front of the Nelms estate. She paused before driving into the circular driveway. "Uhh ... looks like a lot of emergency vehicles and police tape over there. I'll park in the street and we'll walk up."

Wyatt said, "The family said the police had them sitting in the drawing room. Malcolm asked a policeman and he said it would be fine for us to walk in—the police had already investigated over there."

Della answered the door. This time, her smile and dimples were nowhere in evidence. Instead she looked completely exhausted and anxious. She also appeared to have been crying, mascara and eyeliner pooling beneath her eyes.

When Della spotted the bags of food, she burst into tears.

Beatrice looked at Wyatt, alarmed. This was definitely not the desired effect.

He was about to reach out to Della to comfort her when he was beat by Meadow, who fairly tackled Della in the process.

"Della! We're so sorry! And so shocked. We didn't know what to do, so we brought food," said Meadow.

"Come in," murmured Della, breaking free of Meadow's embrace after giving her a small hug in return. She led them into the shadowy light of the drawing room.

It was a lot quieter in the room than it had been the last couple of times they'd been there. Hawkins was sitting on a silk settee, his head in his hands and very still. Malcolm was pacing around the room when they entered. He looked blankly at them at first, then quickly came over and hugged Meadow and Beatrice and extended a hand to Wyatt. It was obvious he hadn't yet shaved for the day and the effect made him look most unlike his usual, well-groomed self. He seemed to recognize this and said, "I actually slept in a bit this morning. I'm regretting that, now. Hearing about ... Sadie ... caught me off-guard even worse that way."

Beatrice said, "That's the last thing you need to be worried about now. But I know what you mean about being caught off-guard. That's a terrible feeling."

Della said in a forced cheerful voice, "They brought some delicious-smelling food."

Malcolm stretched his lips into a smile. "Thank you. I think I might need to save it for a little later. I definitely will need to eat something, but I don't think it's a good idea to force myself to eat yet."

Beatrice said quickly, "It was Meadow's idea, actually. And it's June Bug's baking, so you know it will be a treat when you're ready for it."

Della said, "I'll put it into the kitchen in the meantime. Thanks so much, Meadow."

Malcolm said, "Excuse me for forgetting my manners. Please, sit down."

Wyatt and Beatrice sat down across from Hawkins, who still hadn't looked up at them since they'd come in. Meadow sat in a chair beside Hawkins.

Beatrice mouthed at Malcolm, "Is he all right?"

Malcolm looked at his brother and shrugged a shoulder, shaking his head.

Wyatt cleared his throat and said carefully, "Hawkins? Do you need us to call a doctor for you? I understand that you've had a terrible shock."

Hawkins finally took his head out of his hands. His eyes were bloodshot and half-open. But it looked as if he'd gotten up early and gotten ready. He was clean-shaven and dressed in a navy golf shirt, khaki shorts, and a navy baseball hat.

"No doctor," he said finally. His voice was almost a whisper and Beatrice had to lean forward to hear him.

Beatrice was prepared to leave it there, but this time Hawkins seemed as if he was ready to talk. Maybe he needed to talk it out.

"I was out early," he said, his voice slightly stronger than it had been before. "To see Barkis. He's planning to replant an area of the garden and wanted my opinion on it. The area is going to be surrounded by paving bricks and so forth. I was on my way over when I saw something floating in the lake. You know, the decorative pond that we have out there."

The last sentence sounded more like a question and Beatrice nodded. It was more of a lake than a pond, but she knew what he was talking about.

"I walked out the dock so that I could see better what it was. It was a body." Hawkins shuddered and put his head in his hands again. His voice was muffled as he spoke again. "I could see it was Sadie. I called to Barkis and between the two of us, we somehow got her out." He looked back up at them. "I couldn't leave her like that."

Meadow was openly crying now. "Of course you couldn't!" she said staunchly. She reached over and squeezed his hand.

Malcolm sighed. "Now we'll have the police asking tons of questions again. No offence, Meadow. I know Ramsay would rather be doing anything else than investigating another death."

Meadow nodded. "That he would."

Beatrice asked, "Do you know why Sadie would have been outside like that? Was she usually an early-morning person? Or do you think ..." Her voice trailed off a bit.

"Do we think that she was out there all night in the water?" asked Malcolm, wincing a little. "I'm guessing, unfortunately, that she was out there all night. Sadie was fond of taking a walk after dinner."

Hawkins, still muffled, said, "She was always up early in the mornings, though."

"Yes, but not so much to *walk*. When she was up early in the morning, her habit was to have coffee and breakfast, and catch up on emails," said Malcolm.

Beatrice wondered if her evening walks were enough of a habit that a murderous member of the family might have counted on them as a way of eliminating her.

Della walked back into the drawing room, having dropped off June Bug's food in the kitchen. She had a bit of icing on the corner of her mouth and reached up to wipe it off with a finger. Della sighed. "I couldn't resist June Bug's pecan sticky buns." She sat down next to Malcolm.

Wyatt smiled at her, eyes crinkling. "Who could?"

A minute later, the front door opened and Ramsay stuck his head in. His eyes were sympathetic, but very focused. "Hawkins and Malcolm? Could you both join me for a moment?"

Malcolm stood immediately and frowned at Hawkins until he stood up shakily.

Malcolm said with concern, "Any problems, Ramsay?"

Which made Beatrice grimace a little. Problems other than the massive problem just discovered minutes earlier?

Ramsay nodded. "You've got a very loyal employee in Barkis. But he won't say a blessed word until you both give him the okay."

Malcolm gave a small smile. "That's funny. I don't think Barkis ever cared that much for Hawkins and me. But now that Father is gone, he's apparently transferred his loyalty." He turned to look at Wyatt. "Wyatt, would you mind coming out with us? I'd like to take a few minutes to talk with you about a service for Sadie. And I think I need to get out of this house! Maybe we can talk on the front porch after Hawkins and I speak to Barkis."

"Of course," said Wyatt, standing up.

Malcolm walked out quickly with Wyatt beside him, Hawkins shuffling out behind them.

Della, who'd been smiling brightly and supportively at Malcolm when he was there, slumped as soon as he walked out. Then she burst into tears.

Beatrice rifled through her purse in search of her packet of tissues as Meadow burst into tears herself and hurried over to hug Della. Tears, Beatrice observed, could become a real chain reaction. She finally located the packet and distributed an even amount of tissues to both Della and Meadow.

"I'm so sorry," gasped Della after a few minutes of sobbing had ended. "It's just that Sadie and I were so close. It's such a shock. I've been holding it together for Malcolm, but now that he's not around?" She shook her head wordlessly.

Beatrice nodded at her, although she hadn't really seen any signs that Della and Sadie were all that close.

Meadow asked hesitantly, "Were you here then, when Sadie was discovered?"

Della nodded, miserably. "Yes. Hawkins—well, he was so upset. Malcolm and I couldn't understand a word he was saying at first. Malcolm snapped at him finally and told him to calm down. He was finally able to tell us that he'd found Sadie." She gulped and stopped speaking.

Meadow gave her a sympathetic hug.

Beatrice said, "When was the last time that you saw Sadie last night?" She hoped she didn't sound nosy.

Della didn't seem to find the question nosy at all, or maybe she'd already been asked it by Ramsay. "Last night at dinner. We were eating some food that a few of Caspian's church friends had brought by. We were all just picking at our food, really. Hawkins, especially. Malcolm finally pushed his plate away and said he was too exhausted to eat. And it was super-early, too, but I completely understood what he meant. We hadn't done anything strenuous all day, but it was just the *stress* of Caspian's death that had worn us out."

"You both went up to bed?" asked Beatrice.

Della said with a short laugh. "That's right. At seven-thirty! And I'd like to say that that meant that we were up really early this morning, but that wasn't even true. We must have slept over twelve hours."

"Of course you did!" said Meadow. "After this week? Your bodies clearly needed it."

"We'd just woken up when Hawkins came in," said Della. "I almost wondered if I was still asleep and dreaming the whole thing."

"And you don't have any idea who might be responsible for Sadie's death?" asked Beatrice.

Della raised her eyebrows. "Of course I do. It must be Hawkins."

Chapter Thirteen

Beatrice and Meadow glanced at each other.

"Why would you say that?" asked Beatrice.

Della snorted. "Because Malcolm and I didn't do it. And Sadie is dead. The only person left is Hawkins, unless you think Barkis did it. And why on earth would he do that? This family is his entire life. Besides, Hawkins has been acting strange lately. He's been very erratic with when he eats and when he sleeps. He wanders around at night almost like a ghost. I was relieved when he said that he was going to get up early in the morning and help Barkis because it meant that maybe things were going back to normal. But instead?" Della shrugged. "Who knows how messed up he's going to be now?"

Meadow said with a frown, "So you think that Hawkins is putting on an act about how upset he is? Because if he is, he must be a very good actor."

Della shrugged. "Maybe he's not acting. Maybe he's upset with *himself*. Upset that he lost control and killed Sadie, his own sister."

"But you don't have any proof of that?" asked Beatrice.

"No. But who else could it be?" asked Della.

"Well, after Caspian's death you were fairly positive it must have been Wynona who was responsible," reminded Beatrice.

Della shrugged again. "That's because it made sense. It doesn't make *sense* that Wynona would kill Sadie. They were friends."

"Does it make sense that Hawkins would kill his sister?" asked Meadow skeptically.

"Look, I really have no idea. I'm totally speculating. But it could be that Sadie saw something that made her think that Hawkins was responsible. Maybe she met up with Hawkins last night or this morning or whenever to confront him about it. He could have panicked and killed her," said Della. "All I know is that Sadie is gone. And I can't believe that she won't be my sister anymore." She sobbed.

Beatrice thought that it was a bit premature for Della to think of Sadie as a sister, especially since she wasn't even engaged to Malcolm yet. She also didn't feel much like comforting Della, and was relieved when Meadow came through with another hug.

Meadow also came through with a plug for the Village Quilters. "I tell you what you need," said Meadow in an earnest voice. "You need to get out of this house. This house is just sad and dark right now. You need to come to the guild meeting. Once you sit down with us and create something, you'll feel so much better. Art is so cathartic. And sharing art with others is even more so!"

Della looked dubious. "I'm sure I'd enjoy myself. But I also have to think about Malcolm. Now he's lost half his family and he really needs my support."

"Of course, of course," said Meadow quickly. "Malcolm depends on you, I know. But just keep the guild in the back of your head in case you want to do something completely distracting. Because the guild is distracting, isn't it, Beatrice."

"I'll say," said Beatrice dryly.

"Thanks," said Della with a smile. "I'll keep it in mind." Her eyes opened wide. "I wonder if we'll be able to have the service tomorrow, after all. We were planning on having Caspian's funeral tomorrow afternoon. But now, with all this?"

Beatrice said, "As hard as it is to imagine, it might be best for the family to just go ahead with that plan. It might be easier to deal with Sadie's death after putting Caspian to rest. Having at least a little closure before trying to handle Sadie's death and service."

Della thought about this for a moment and then nodded. "I'll mention that to Malcolm. I'm sure he'll be the one taking over planning Sadie's funeral. Hawkins isn't going to be any help." She gave a sudden short laugh. "And at least we all know what type of service Sadie would have wanted! She made that pretty clear when we were all trying to plan Caspian's funeral. Hopefully, Malcolm is remembering that while he's talking with Wyatt outside. And with any luck, Hawkins isn't try-ing to push some sort of modern service again."

The front door pushed open and Hawkins stumbled through in tears. He collapsed into a chair, head back in his hands.

Della gave Beatrice and Meadow a look. "I'm going outside with Malcolm and Wyatt," she announced. When she passed Beatrice, she leaned over and muttered, "Please see what you can do with Hawkins. He's a disaster."

Beatrice wished that Wyatt had come back in. She felt a little help-less when dealing with disasters.

Fortunately, Meadow got up and sat down in the chair next to Hawkins. She patted his knee. "You've had such a shock this morning. Do you want me to get you something? A coffee or something to eat?"

Hawkins lifted his head and looked hopefully at her. "A drink?"

Meadow looked startled. "A drink? Well ... sure. Okay. It's five o'clock somewhere, right? I'll go in the kitchen and rustle something up."

She left the room and Beatrice said, "Things will start looking up soon. You've just had two big shocks right after the other. People are worried about you."

"People?" asked Hawkins. A glimpse of curiosity crossed his fea-tures.

"Well, Della, for one. And Malcolm, too," said Beatrice.

Hawkins looked less-interested and shrugged a shoulder. "Family," he muttered.

Beatrice said, "As a matter of fact, *not* just family. Wynona is help-ing me with my wedding—I don't know if you knew that. She asked me specially to come over and make sure that you're all right."

Now Beatrice had Hawkins' full attention. "Really? She brought me up?"

"Not only did she bring you up, but she was worried about you." Beatrice paused. "I understand that you and Wynona broke up because of family reasons. But I know when I'm going through a rough time, having a friend to talk to really helps."

Hawkins sat very still, considering this. "But I broke up with her. And then ... well, I wasn't the best person when she tried to get back together with me. My father, you know. He didn't approve of Wynona. Long ago he'd had an argument with Wynona's father. Not only that, but he had some sort of dream of me marrying someone who'd bring more wealth into the family—a first son marrying well scenario. It was ridiculous, and I told him so. But he was a stubborn man. I didn't get anywhere with him by arguing. I ended the relationship."

Beatrice said gently, "But Wynona didn't accept that, did she?"

Hawkins shook his head. "She knew that I still cared for her. And she still cared for me. When I didn't take her calls, she'd drop by." He sighed. "She'd be chased off by Father or Barkis or someone. She was persistent for a while, but then she stopped coming."

"Wynona is clearly still thinking about you," said Beatrice. "She must have some feelings still for you."

Hawkins shook his head again. "I don't see how," he said slowly. He thought for a moment and then repeated sadly, "I don't see how. I've made so many mistakes."

"Why don't you reach out to her? Leave it up to her?" asked Beatrice. "If you don't give her the chance to decide whether she wants to have a relationship with you again, then you're making the decision for both of you. And that's not really fair."

Hawkins sighed. "You're right, you're right. Of course you're right. I just hate that when I finally reach out to her, it's because I need something. Or someone. But this has been so horrible ... what's been happening." He gave an even bigger sigh. "I've been such a screw-up. I don't think I've done anything right. I've wasted my father's money. I've not been able to find any decent employment. I haven't been able to sustain a relationship." He gave a short laugh. "And now I'm a suspect in two different murder investigations."

Meadow came bustling back in. "Well, *that* took a while. Sorry. I didn't realize that y'all kept your liquor in a special cabinet. I was pawing through the pantry as if you kept your alcohol in the same spots we do."

Hawkins took the drink from Meadow and then said with a small smile. "And, after all that trouble, I think I'm going to decline your drink. It's morning. I need to hold on better than I'm doing right now. I'll be okay without it." He stood up and put the glass on a table across the room before sitting back down.

"Would you like to talk about it? What happened this morning?" asked Beatrice hesitantly.

He paused for a moment and then nodded quickly. "I think so. Maybe it would help to get the images out of my head. Of Sadie just floating there." He shuddered.

Beatrice said, "I understand you were up early this morning? Something to do with Barkis?"

Hawkins looked grateful at the prompt. "That's right. I was trying to get back into the swing of things. Trying to keep my head screwed on straight. Besides, Barkis needed to know what to do with some projects he's working on. Before, he'd have just asked Father, but now—I needed to step in. I told him I'd be up early this morning and we'd look at it together. He likes to work early before it starts getting too hot outside."

"And you walked by the lake?" asked Beatrice.

"That's right. I passed a section of the grounds where Barkis was putting up pavers. There was a wheelbarrow there with paving bricks and then there were a couple on the ground. I thought the ones on the ground were kind of weird because Barkis is always so deliberate with everything he does. I glanced around to see if there was anything else out of place." Hawkins hesitated. "Then something in the water caught my eye." He took a deep breath.

Meadow said with feeling, "You poor thing. After the week you've had!"

He said, "I knew it was Sadie. And I knew that something must have *happened* to her. It wasn't as if Sadie would have gone swimming in the lake. Even if she had, she's a strong swimmer. I called Barkis first, though, before I called the police. I just couldn't *leave* her in the lake. Barkis and I pulled her out." He gave a short laugh. "And obviously I didn't have an alibi since I was the one who found her. I'm sure the police are going to love that."

Beatrice said, "But what about last night? It sounds as if Sadie usually took walks at night and not early in the morning?"

Hawkins said, "That's no help, either. I couldn't sleep, so I was on my computer in my room for hours. No one saw me." He sighed. "This is just so tragic. I loved Sadie, I really did. I mean, we would have stupid arguments, of course. We were brother and sister, after all. But growing up, we spent tons of time together, being closest in age. We used to stand up to Father together. That is, *Sadie* probably stood up to Father better than I did."

"Malcolm said that you seemed to be standing up to your father quite a bit more in the last couple of months," said Beatrice. "At least, that he heard you arguing."

Hawkins nodded. "I'd started to realize what a terrible mistake I'd made by listening to Father and ending my relationship with Wynona. As that became more and more obvious, I argued more and more with him about the control he was taking in my life. Control that he'd bought, in a way."

Meadow said, "No wonder you've been looking so anxious lately. You've had a lot on your mind!"

Hawkins said, "I have. And now I'm feeling so guilty on top of everything else. I actually believed that Sadie might be responsible for our father's death. That was just me slinging out wild accusations. She obviously had nothing to do with it. I see that, now."

Beatrice asked, "Who do you think might be responsible for this?"

Hawkins blew out a big gust of a sigh. "I'm wondering if it could have been Malcolm. Oh, but I really hate to speculate, since that got me in trouble last time. But every time I overhear Malcolm talking about Father's death, he seems to be intimating that it has something to do with me. That *I* was the one who was arguing so much with Father—that our relationship had soured enough that I might consider somehow getting rid of him. Even you were saying that Malcolm had brought up our arguing."

"You're wondering if maybe Malcolm is blaming you to divert attention from himself?" asked Beatrice.

Hawkins shrugged. "Maybe."

Beatrice said, "Della said that she and Malcolm were just waking up when you came back to tell them about Sadie."

Hawkins raised his eyebrows. "Really? Because he sure didn't look as if he'd just woken up to me. He was very alert." He sighed. "I can't believe Sadie is gone. She was so good ... nothing like me. I was always worried about all the wrong things while Sadie was out trying to save the world, do good deeds, pursue social work, whatever. She was still talking about justice to me even yesterday."

"What was she saying?" asked Beatrice.

"She said that Father was dead for the wrong reasons."

"But that makes it sound as though she knew who was responsible for your father's death," said Beatrice slowly.

At that moment, the front door opened again and Malcolm and Wyatt came in. Hawkins stopped talking and looked back down at the floor.

Wyatt said, "We've gotten some basic plans set for a service for Sadie—and we're keeping Caspian's tomorrow, as scheduled."

Beatrice stood up. As soon as Malcolm walked in through the door, she felt tension in the room. "We should probably be going," she said quickly.

Meadow stood up too and gave more hugs to Hawkins and Malcolm. "We're so, so sorry. Would you like me to bring food tomorrow?" she asked.

Malcolm said with a smile, "You've already done so much, Meadow, thank you. Besides, after Father's service tomorrow, we'll probably have plenty of leftover food."

Wyatt said, "I'll make sure that the ladies at the church know that the service is still set for tomorrow. And yes, you should have *plenty* of leftover food. They do a wonderful job."

They walked out of the house and Wyatt carefully closed the door behind them. He grimaced at Beatrice. "I hate that they've had another tragedy there in such a short period of time," he said in a low voice.

Meadow gave a gusty sigh. "Isn't that the truth?" She looked over the yard and saw Ramsay in the distance, behind police tape. He had a group of state police officers around him, surveying the scene. "I suppose Ramsay will be working late again." She squinted and then stopped completely, peering into the distance. "What's that?"

"What's what?" asked Beatrice.

Meadow gasped. "I think ... well, take a look over there and tell me what *you* see."

Beatrice and Wyatt stopped too, frowning and looking into the distance.

"Is that ... could that be *Maisie*?" asked Beatrice.

Chapter Fourteen

Meadow started jogging toward the cat. "It's got to be! She's wearing a crocheted sweater!"

Beatrice said in alarm, "Wait! Hold on, Meadow, you're going to scare her off."

"But Maisie is always so laid back," scoffed Meadow. "She should be glad to see us."

Wyatt said, "Beatrice is probably right, Meadow. Maisie might still be a little freaked out by being outside. Besides, there are all these people here and a lot of commotion. Let's approach her really cautiously so she won't run off."

Maisie was indeed skittish. She hesitated at first when they got within a few yards of her, but then bolted off.

Meadow was desperately scrabbling in her purse. "Surely I've got some food in here that we could lure her with. That's *definitely* Maisie. Oh, Miss Sissy is going to be so relieved!" She pulled out a pack of crackers that looked as those it might have been in the bottom of Meadow's purse for a while as if Maisie's prolonged stint in the great outdoors might have changed her from a carnivore to a cracker eater.

Wyatt frowned, tracking the cat with his eyes. "It looks as if she's heading past the police tape."

"What? Well, we'll just have to go in there. It's an emergency. Ramsay will understand," said Meadow huffily.

Beatrice wasn't at all sure that Ramsay *would* understand. "Let's walk up to the tape and tell him what's going on. Maybe one of the guys can grab Maisie while she's distracted. There are enough people and commotion to distract her. Maybe she's simply curious. She's hiding under that bush where she can see them, but they can't see her."

Meadow stomped toward Ramsay. "I'll tell Ramsay to get her," she said grimly.

Wyatt and Beatrice glanced at each other. "It's not like Ramsay has anything else going on," said Beatrice with a laugh. "Not like a new murder investigation, or anything."

Wyatt's eyes were focused on Maisie. "The good news is that the cat doesn't look as if she's about to dash off again. I don't think she knows we've seen her."

Beatrice laughed again as Meadow, hands on her hips and looking her bossiest, talked to Ramsay. Ramsay was shaking his head in response to whatever Meadow was saying, but then gave a small shrug and turned around to follow where Meadow was pointing.

"I guess Maisie trumps the murder investigation," said Wyatt, smiling.

"*Meadow* trumps the murder investigation. If Ramsay had just ignored her, he'd never have heard the end of it," said Beatrice.

They watched, holding their breaths, as Ramsay strode toward the bush, bent abruptly, and picked up (none-too-gently) the white cat wearing the sweater, and placed it in Meadow's arms.

Meadow, beaming and clutching the cat fiercely, hurried back toward Wyatt and Beatrice.

"It's Maisie all right!" she crowed. "Let's get her in the car before she escapes again!"

"Aren't you holding her just a little too tightly?" asked Beatrice. "We do want the cat to be able to breathe, you know."

"I'm not taking any chances on Maisie getting away again," said Meadow.

They started the long walk back to the car, Maisie looking alarmed and Beatrice trying to calm her down by telling her what a good cat she was. Even though Beatrice believed quite the opposite about Maisie's overall behavior during the incident.

Wyatt said, "Miss Sissy is going to be over the moon."

"If we can *find* Miss Sissy. For all we know, she's out in the woods, looking for the cat." But Beatrice smiled, looking forward to the old woman's reaction.

Sure enough, there was no answer when they knocked at Miss Sissy's door.

"I'll try her cell phone," said Meadow. She shook her head a minute later. "No answer."

Beatrice said, "Before we go any further, let's put Maisie in a carrier. She's looking pretty anxious right now and the last thing we need is for her to run off again."

"Boris has one we can borrow," said Meadow quickly.

Beatrice said, "No, let's grab Noo-noo's. Boris's is so big that it probably won't even fit in the car."

Meadow drove the short distance to Beatrice's and she ran in, getting the crate and an old towel to line the bottom of it. Maisie seemed to appreciate the crate, looking a lot more relaxed when she was safely inside.

"Now we can start looking for Miss Sissy," said Wyatt.

"First, we're looking for a cat, then we're looking for a cat owner," said Beatrice, shaking her head. "I'm not sure which is harder."

They drove slowly past the woods around Beatrice's and Meadow's houses. Then they drove to the park where there was a small lake, trails, and a wooded area. There was no sign of her.

Meadow said with a sigh, "Well, I guess we can always head back over near the Nelms estate. That's the only place left that we haven't driven past."

"And we can have the opportunity to irritate Ramsay once again today," said Beatrice. "Who wants to pass that up?"

Wyatt said, "Regardless, I think we should probably drive over. We don't have to get close to the police tape. I hate the thought of her still being so worried and out looking for Maisie the whole day."

As it happened, they didn't have to get up close to Ramsay's area at all. They saw Miss Sissy's dilapidated old Lincoln in the circular drive-way, and the old woman, who appeared to have half a bird's nest in her hair, was limping toward it, looking exhausted.

"She's so dejected! Oh hurry, Beatrice, jump out and show her we've got Maisie!" said Meadow in agitation.

Beatrice waited a couple of seconds for Wyatt to stop the car, not being eager to jump out of a moving vehicle, and immediately called out "Miss Sissy! We've got Maisie!"

The old woman stopped in her tracks, gaping at them in disbelief. Then she galloped toward them in a speedy, limping gait, face lit up with joy, exhaustion forgotten.

Beatrice quickly set down the carrier and called out to Meadow and Wyatt. "Backup needed! I think Maisie's coming out of the crate!"

Sure enough, Miss Sissy was immediately on the crate, opening the latch and gathering the cat up close to her. A tear ran down either cheek as she crooned to the animal softly. Beatrice didn't ordinarily think of cats as particularly affectionate, but Maisie was proving her wrong as she rubbed her face repeatedly against Miss Sissy's.

Meadow was smiling through her tears. Wyatt even wiped away a tear of his own. Beatrice gave Miss Sissy a hug, but then decided Miss Sissy might be better served by having the bird nest removed from her hair. She carefully removed the twigs and moss as Miss Sissy continued holding Maisie tightly and crooning to her.

"Where did you find her?" asked Miss Sissy gruffly.

"We were all walking out of the Nelms house this morning when Meadow spotted her. We drove to my house to get Noo-noo's carrier, and then looked for you," said Beatrice. "Meadow tried to call you on your cell phone."

"Didn't bring it," said the old woman. Then she looked smug. "*Knew* Maisie was over here. People kept saying they spotted her out this way."

Beatrice, still leery that Maisie would get spooked again and head back out for another adventure in the woods, said, "Let's get you both back home."

Wyatt said, "How about if I drive Miss Sissy's car back so that she can visit with Maisie on the way back?"

"Good idea," said Beatrice. Anything to get the cat back into the car and safely back to Miss Sissy's house. She gently took Maisie from Miss Sissy. "She seemed much calmer and happier when she was in the crate in the car."

Miss Sissy nodded and clambered into the van. Beatrice swung the carrier in next to the old woman and they started up the engine.

"I'll call Posy and let her know that Maisie is found," said Meadow, pulling slowly out of the driveway behind Wyatt.

Wyatt appeared to be driving even slower than usual. This was probably due to the fact that he was concerned the ancient Lincoln might self-destruct at any second.

Miss Sissy had stuck as many of her fingers as possible through the bars of the carrier and was petting Maisie, who looked very pleased.

Beatrice said, "Miss Sissy, you said that you'd heard reports that Maisie was over near the Nelms estate. Did you look over there yourself?"

"Of course," scoffed the old woman. "All the time."

"All the time? Were you there before we found you this morning?" asked Beatrice.

"Was there last night," said Miss Sissy as if staying out all night looking for a cat made perfect sense.

"Did you see Sadie last night? Sadie Nelms?" asked Beatrice.

Meadow took in a deep breath as if the weight of the universe rested on Miss Sissy's answer.

Miss Sissy frowned reprovingly at Meadow for the noise, which startled Maisie. Then she said to Beatrice. "Nope. Saw Wynona."

Meadow turned to stare at Beatrice and Beatrice yelped, "Meadow, the road!"

Meadow swerved to get back on the road again.

Miss Sissy was looking most reproachfully now at Meadow. "Road hog!"

Beatrice said in a coaxing voice, "Miss Sissy, try to think. What time did you see Wynona?"

"Time?" The old woman stared at Beatrice as if the passing of time was an aspect of life that had very little relevance to her.

Beatrice noticed that there was no watch present on Miss Sissy's wrist. She said, "All right, then. Was it dark then?"

The old woman nodded. "Dark."

"How dark?" pressed Beatrice.

"Pretty darn dark," snarled Miss Sissy, losing patience with the questions.

Apparently, any points that Beatrice and Meadow had scored with Miss Sissy by finding and returning the wayward Maisie were rapidly being depleted.

Meadow said, "You see, Miss Sissy, Sadie was murdered last night. We're trying to find out who might be responsible. You remember Sadie, don't you? She was at the party we threw for Beatrice. You seemed to like her."

Miss Sissy grunted noncommittally.

"You'd be doing us a great favor if you could tell us anything you remember. We know you were focusing on Maisie, but did you maybe talk to Wynona? You must have been surprised to see her out there in the dark," said Meadow in a wheedling tone.

Beatrice asked, "Did Wynona see *you*, Miss Sissy?"

"Course she did," snapped the old woman. "I was out there calling, wasn't I?"

"Did she say anything to you about why she was there?" asked Beatrice.

"Said she was helping look for the cat," muttered Miss Sissy.

That would likely have been the end of the questions from Miss Sissy for Wynona. If she thought Wynona was helping to look for Maisie, she would simply have accepted that at face value. To Miss Sissy, it was natural that *everyone* would have helped to find her missing cat. If it was important to Miss Sissy, it followed that it was important for everyone else.

"What was her mood? Did she seem anxious? Quiet?" asked Beatrice.

Miss Sissy glared at her. "Seemed like she was looking for a cat."

This seemed to be the end of the road on the subject. Wyatt pulled Miss Sissy's boat of a car into her driveway and Meadow followed behind.

"I'll carry the crate for you," said Beatrice, but Miss Sissy had already picked it up with surprising alacrity, and was trotting up the driveway to her front door. A minute later, she gently scooped Maisie out of the carrier, deposited her inside, and shoved the crate out the door. She gave a quick, unenthusiastic wave before slamming the door behind her.

Wyatt walked up to their window. "I'm going to walk back to the house. I think I need a few minutes to clear my head."

"I don't blame you," said Beatrice with a sigh. "I feel the same way. I'll check in with you later."

"Well, I guess that's that," said Meadow as she pulled out of Miss Sissy's driveway. "Posy sure was glad to hear the news about Maisie. I have a feeling that Miss Sissy will be having a visitor later." She paused. "You don't think that Wynona had anything to do with Sadie's murder, surely. They were good friends."

"But what was she doing out there at night?" asked Beatrice.

"We'll just have to ask her. I'm sure she'll have a good explanation. I certainly hope that the best florist in town isn't a murderer. That would leave us high and dry for a couple of upcoming weddings, wouldn't it? And I have the feeling that my efforts at flower arranging wouldn't prove to be much of a substitute," said Meadow with a sigh. "Maybe we can at least figure out she's a murderer *after* she's finished with the weddings."

Beatrice said, "I need to talk to her."

"About the flowers?"

"Unfortunately, no. The flowers would have been a good excuse, but we're all squared away with them, I think." Then Beatrice snapped her fingers. "Wynona *did* say that she wanted for her dog, Watson, and Noo-noo to have a playdate. I think today might be the perfect time. Besides, that way I can maybe catch her off-guard. The news of Sadie's death probably hasn't made it around town yet. I could see her reaction in person."

Meadow said, "I didn't realize Wynona had a dog."

"She didn't—not until a couple of weeks ago. She's got a Labradoodle puppy with endless supplies of energy, apparently. She was hoping Noo-noo could help her puppy deplete some of his energy," said Beatrice. She grimaced. "Of course, now I've got *two* dogs on my hands. But I'm pretty sure I can handle only one of them for a playdate."

Meadow laughed. "I wonder if her puppy is going to be too much for Noo-noo. She should set up a playdate with Boris, instead! Noo-noo will probably be worn out for the rest of the day."

Beatrice smiled. "You're right. But for some reason she chose Noo-noo ... I guess because of her size."

Meadow pulled into Beatrice's driveway. "Well, let me know what you find out. Remember your crate!"

Beatrice walked in, setting down the crate by the door and sitting down to rub Noo-noo for a few minutes. Finally, she picked up her phone.

"Wynona? It's Beatrice. I was wondering if you'd like to meet up at the park? I thought today might be a great day for the dogs to play. Now? That's perfect. See you in a few."

Fifteen minutes later, Beatrice and Noo-noo were at the park. They walked toward the lake and immediately spotted Wynona waving at them and her tan colored Labradoodle grinning at them and leaping around on his leash.

"I'm so glad you called!" said Wynona. "Watson got up at five this morning and has been going like a house on fire ever since. Maybe Noo-noo can take some of the energy out of him."

She looked so pleased that Beatrice felt a little guilty about her plan. But not guilty enough not to go through with it. She smiled back and said, "Want to sit down on the bench by the lake and let them play? I've got Noo-noo on a long leash and I brought an extra one in case you didn't have one yet."

Wynona looked grateful. "That would be great, if I could borrow that. It should be easier for them to play that way."

The women sat down and laughed for a few minutes, watching the dogs play. Beatrice was glad to see that Noo-noo was very patient with the puppy and didn't seem to mind all the nips. In fact, the little dog appeared to be having a great time. Maybe she had needed a little playtime, too.

Beatrice said, "Noo-noo's loving this. And I am, too. I think I needed a distraction after this morning."

Wynona, who'd been smiling at Watson, looked swiftly over at Beatrice. "This morning? What happened this morning?"

Beatrice took a deep breath. "Wynona, I'm sorry to have to tell you this, but Sadie Nelms died last night. She was murdered."

Chapter Fifteen

Wynona gasped, turning white. "What? But—that's impossible. I just talked to her yesterday."

Beatrice nodded. "I knew it would be a shock to you. I'm sorry. I know the two of you were good friends."

Tears flowed down Wynona's cheeks. "Friends, yes. But I didn't have enough time with her. She'd just recently moved back home to make up with her father. Why would somebody do something like this?"

Beatrice shook her head. "No one knows. I can only guess that maybe she knew something about her father's killer—something that the murderer didn't want to get out. Maybe she was silenced." She paused. "There's something I want to ask you about. We found Miss Sissy's cat, Maisie. While we were returning it to her, she said that she'd seen you at the Nelms estate last night."

Wynona turned even whiter. "Miss Sissy must have been confused," she stammered.

"I'm afraid not," said Beatrice gently. "Despite Miss Sissy's some-what erratic mental state, she seemed very certain."

Wynona looked down at the ground, blindly staring at the two dogs, happily playing. She said slowly, "She was right. I was there last night."

Beatrice waited for a moment, not wanting to push her. Finally, Wynona continued, "I was there with Watson, actually. I was walking him." She gave a short, harsh laugh. "Actually, I was just walking him for pretense. I was hoping that maybe Hawkins would see me and come out of the house to talk. Or that maybe he'd be walking around on the grounds and I could see him. After all the rejections, I guess that maybe I'm too gun-shy to ring the doorbell, even if Caspian is gone."

"Did he come out?" asked Beatrice.

Wynona made a face. "He didn't. Which made me sad, because I'd actually paid special attention to my hair and makeup before going on my walk."

Beatrice said, "Did you see anyone?"

Wynona nodded slowly. "I sure did. I saw Malcolm."

Beatrice frowned. "Just making sure again—this was last night? And it was getting dark?"

Wynona nodded again.

Beatrice said, "That's very interesting, since Malcolm said that he was in bed, asleep, right after an early dinner."

"He certainly wasn't," said Wynona with a snort. "Not unless he was walking in his sleep."

"And yet Della gave him an alibi," said Beatrice thoughtfully, watching as Noo-noo rolled over on her back as Watson licked her face.

"Well, of course she did. He's her ticket to a better life, isn't he? She's going to stand by him no matter what. But if you ask me, I think Malcolm must know something," said Wynona.

"What makes you so sure?" asked Beatrice.

"He looked very stressed out. He was frowning and his face was simply thunderous. I figured that Barkis had done something stupid and he was irritated about that. Malcolm is pretty protective over the estate and he can be a real perfectionist," said Wynona.

Beatrice asked, "Did you say anything to him?"

Wynona laughed. "Are you kidding? I didn't want to attract any attention at all. I wasn't supposed to be there, remember? I didn't want to give Malcolm an excuse to throw me off the estate. Watson and I slipped into the woods."

They both sat quietly for a few minutes, watching the dogs —Wynona seemingly trying to wrap her head around Sadie's death and Beatrice absorbing the fact that Malcolm had lied to her about where he was the night before.

Wynona finally broke the silence. "I wanted to ask you something and please tell me your real opinion."

Beatrice nodded.

"Do you think it's appropriate for me to go to Caspian's funeral tomorrow? Or not? I know everybody realizes I wasn't exactly Caspian's biggest fan, but I want to show my support for the family ... well, Hawkins in particular." Wynona flushed becomingly. "Do you think that my presence there would be completely inappropriate under the circumstances?"

Beatrice said gently, "I think the family would appreciate the gesture. Especially Hawkins."

"I'll just make sure to wear something unobtrusive and stand near the back," said Wynona. "I feel so sorry for them. First their father, then their sister."

The dogs came trotting back to them, panting, their tongues hanging out of their mouths. Wynona laughed as they fished in their bags for water and a collapsible bowl. "Thanks for letting Watson play with Noo-noo, Beatrice. I have the feeling that he's going to be sleeping very well tonight."

Beatrice smiled back, but wasn't so sure that *she* was going to be sleeping very well. There was too much going on in her head. For the rest of the hour, she and Wynona talked about the wedding and small talk. But the whole time, Beatrice felt like half of her mind was thinking about Sadie's death.

After Beatrice returned home, she called June Bug. It went right to her voice mail, which wasn't surprising—when June Bug was working, she was *working*.

After five o'clock rolled around, Beatrice's phone rang.

June Bug asked in her worried tone, "Would now be all right to run by and meet your dog? I told the sitter that I'd be home a little later."

"Now is perfect. Come on by."

When June Bug knocked on the door, Noo-noo was up and greeting her immediately ... and so was Scooter. The dog grinned at June Bug and nuzzled her hand when she stretched it out to him. Beatrice watched as the stress and worry on June Bug's face melted away and she smiled at Scooter. Scooter responded by immediately flopping over onto his back for a tummy rub.

June Bug's eyes lit up. "Beatrice, I think he's perfect. Katy said she'd always wanted a dog, but her mother wouldn't let her have one. I didn't tell her about Scooter in case it didn't work out. But he's great."

Beatrice said warmly, "He's all yours, if you want him. The owner said he'd had all his shots and was fixed. I think he'll make a wonderful pet for Katy."

June Bug nodded. "Think maybe she'll talk to him? Maybe he'll give her a little comfort. Katy and I are still trying to get to know each other and she could use a dog who just—loves her."

Beatrice chuckled. "I bet whenever Katy comes home from school that Scooter will be there wagging his tail like crazy."

June Bug said, "I've got it all figured out, too. I've got a back room that's an office that Scooter can hang out in. I can't keep him in the bakery part because of Health Department rules, but he can stay in the office and I can visit with him. Then Katy can come play with him when she's out of school." She looked at her watch and said sadly, "And now I've got to go, Beatrice. Sorry."

Beatrice had the feeling that June Bug really wanted to spend some time with another adult. She must have been under a lot of stress lately with her sister's death and Katy's arrival. "Why don't I run by tomorrow morning for a visit? We can catch up a little and I can see how things with Scooter went overnight. And I've had a craving for your pastries lately, too.

June Bug beamed at her and nodded shyly. And she kept on smiling as she and Scooter hurried off home.

The next morning, Beatrice woke up very early. She gave up trying to sleep and got dressed. June Bug's bakery in downtown Dappled Hills opened very early, she knew. She only hoped it was *this* early. She decided to walk down there.

Beatrice was so engrossed in her thoughts that she was surprised when she got to June Bug's shop—she didn't even remember her walk over. She glanced at her watch. What's more, she'd gotten here in record time and wasn't really even out of breath.

Beatrice saw with relief that there was an open sign on June Bug's door. She walked in and June Bug scurried out from the back of the store, beaming when she saw Beatrice.

"Good morning!" she said with a shy smile. "You're up early."

"Not as early as you, I'm thinking," said Beatrice with a wry smile. "You'll make me feel better about my lack of sleep last night if you tell me when you got up this morning."

"Four o'clock," said June Bug, her eyes dancing.

"Thank you," said Beatrice. "I now feel better rested. Although I still need a strong coffee. And something very sugary to eat. Maybe that pastry there."

June Bug gave her a bright smile and quickly poured Beatrice a full cup of coffee. She carefully put the pastry on a plate and checked Beatrice out.

"Thanks, June Bug," said Beatrice, sitting down at a table. She pulled out several napkins, having the feeling that she was going to need them, considering the lack of sleep. "Let me know if you need to get back to your baking—I know mornings are your busy time."

June Bug perched on a chair across from Beatrice and smiled at her. "I have some time," she said. "Thanks again for Scooter."

"What did Katy think?" asked Beatrice.

"She was *so* excited. She absolutely loved him. And, for the first time since she's been with me, she really started *talking*," said June Bug, her eyes bright.

"That's wonderful! That's exactly what we hoped would happen," said Beatrice.

June Bug nodded. "Katy talked to Scooter and then talked to me *about* Scooter. Then, after a while, she talked with me a little about her mom." June Bug looked more somber now. "She's been really missing her."

"Of course! She was Mom. That's only natural. But the important thing is, June Bug, that Katy knows you love her and are making a home for her," said Beatrice. "Scooter will be the first of what will be a lot of new friends for her, I'm sure."

June Bug said, "I hope so. But tell me what's happening with you, Beatrice. You seemed worried when you walked in."

Beatrice sighed. "My mind has been spinning. There's been so much going on. Did you hear about Sadie yesterday?"

June Bug nodded, her large, protruding eyes troubled. She said, "There's a funeral today?"

"There's *Caspian's* funeral today. Early this afternoon. I'm not sure when Sadie's is."

June Bug said sadly, "It's a mess. But you have a wedding coming up. You need to remember to be happy."

Beatrice thought about this for a few moments as she took a satisfying sip of the French roast coffee June Bug had made for her. June Bug was right. There was a lot of wisdom in the little woman, although frequently Beatrice suspected that she was just too shy to deliver it. Beatrice had been allowing the stress of wedding planning and the activities surrounding the wedding to stress her out. Not only that, but she'd allowed her sadness over the events at the Nelms estate to overwhelm her more positive emotions. And when she thought of her married life with Wyatt, the first thing that came to mind was the moving and combining of two households.

Beatrice made a face. "June Bug, you're right. I think I'll relax a lot more if I can focus on what's coming down the line. Wyatt and I are getting married! And everything else will work out. It will definitely be busy. And I'm determined to help Ramsay figure out what's happening at the Nelms estate. But ultimately, I need to just look ahead to the future."

June Bug said gently, "You and Wyatt make such a nice couple. It makes me happy to see the two of you together." She glanced up as the door opened and then smiled and swiftly got up, bustling away without another word.

Beatrice took a bite of her pastry and then turned to see who'd come in.

It was Wyatt, whose eyes brightened as he saw her. "Beatrice! But it's so early."

Beatrice nodded. "I couldn't sleep. Could you?"

He shook his head. "No. And then I was thinking about Caspian's service today and just decided to get up. But do you know what's helping me this morning, with the stress?"

Beatrice shook her head.

"Thinking of you," he said, eyes crinkling.

"Me too," said Beatrice, a bit nonsensically. And then, "Is it too early for cupcakes? I'm thinking we should both have a white cupcake. A preview for the wedding cake," she added with a smile.

And they did.

That afternoon, Beatrice rode with Meadow to Caspian's funeral since Wyatt was going very early.

"Are we going to be able to see Wyatt after the funeral at all?" asked Meadow on the way over.

"I'm afraid not. He's got hospital visits right afterward, so he'll be leaving very soon after the service is over," said Beatrice.

Meadow glanced across at Beatrice. "How are you doing? It seemed like Sadie's death hit you like it did me. You know, I felt a real connection with her and it wasn't just the quilting. It was as if she was finally living her life and really doing what she wanted to do—she was a social worker and came back home to make up with her father."

Beatrice nodded. "Her father, who was disappointed in her and in Hawkins, too. Yes, her death did hit me hard. But I'm getting a little distanced from it now, I think."

Meadow raised her eyebrows. "How are you managing that?"

"June Bug reminded me that I have something very life-affirming coming up soon. I'm joining my life with Wyatt's. And so, even though I was distressed by Sadie's death, I'm trying to put everything in perspective. Instead of being upset, I'm channeling my feelings into being focused on finding out who did it," said Beatrice. She surprised herself by her steely voice.

Meadow definitely approved. "That's it! Let's get him. For Sadie. A quilting sister!"

"Did Ramsay say anything else yesterday? Any more information about Sadie's death or any evidence at all?"

Meadow made a face. "Not really. He came home really exhausted last night. The only thing I could get out of him was that *everybody's* footprints were out near Sadie. The entire household. There wasn't anything that pointed to any one person. She was definitely hit over the head and then pushed into the water. They found a paving brick that was the weapon."

Meadow pulled into the cemetery and parked. She frowned. "What time is it? I thought we were here early."

"We *are* here early," said Beatrice, staring at the crowd already gathered at the graveside. "But apparently most of the town decided to come to Caspian's funeral."

"What on earth!" said Meadow indignantly. "I wouldn't have said he had this many close friends. Do you think they're just curious?"

"Unfortunately, his death does make quite an interesting story. A wealthy, irascible old man in a mansion, who is murdered by someone in his own home, and right before a party. And now his daughter has died under mysterious circumstances. I'm sure people are curious," said Beatrice.

"Well, people are morbid," said Meadow, glaring at the assembled group. Then she paused, right before opening her door. "Wait. Is that Wynona there? I'm surprised to see her here. She didn't think this was *Sadie's* funeral, did she?"

"Of course not! She asked me if I thought it was appropriate for her to be here and I told her yes. After all, she's showing support for the family, especially Hawkins," said Beatrice.

"People will probably talk," said Meadow thoughtfully. "But then, they're going to talk anyway. And Hawkins keeps glancing over at her—look."

It did seem as though Hawkins' eyes were drawn to Wynona. Wynona was definitely not trying to stand out and was dressed in somber attire and standing off to the side. Still, Hawkins couldn't seem to take his eyes off her.

"It's probably good to have something to distract him," said Beatrice.

"True. His eyes are totally bloodshot. I wonder if he's remembered to have anything to eat. And we brought all that good food over! If that doesn't tempt him, nothing will," said Meadow.

They joined the group by the graveside, standing somewhat to the side. Wyatt spotted Beatrice and gave her a small nod and smile.

The service was exactly the compromise that Sadie and Hawkins settled on: a mix of traditional and contemporary. Malcolm gave the eulogy, and it was full of both wry humor and sad memories. Della, wearing a black suit, watched him with a proud smile. Wyatt, as usual, did a wonderful job balancing the tragic nature of a funeral with the uplifting nature of eternal life.

Meadow touched her eyes with a tissue. "He did a good job," she whispered.

After a closing hymn, the service was over. Hawkins and Malcolm were swarmed by the gathered mourners.

"Let's go stand with Wynona. She's looking like she feels out of place," said Beatrice.

Wynona smiled at them as they walked up.

"I'm glad you made it," said Beatrice.

"I am, too," said Wynona, "although it was tough to convince myself this morning to come. Still, I feel like I'm giving Hawkins a show of support." She shook her head. "He looks terrible, doesn't he?"

"It's all really hit him hard," said Meadow. "But he sure looked glad to see you here, Wynona."

Wynona colored a bit. "I guess we should head off now?"

"Certainly not! We should stay and talk to the family for a minute," said Meadow stoutly. "There's no reason to run off and hide."

They took a seat on a bench nearby and waited for the line to recede. "There are quite a lot of stragglers at this funeral," said Beatrice with a frown at all the groups of people still talking with each other instead of leaving the cemetery.

Meadow shrugged. "Sometimes, the only way to catch up with people is at weddings and funerals, it seems like."

"At least it finally looks like the family has spoken to everyone," said Beatrice. "Should we walk over?"

Wynona gave a startled gasp. "Oh! It looks like ... is Hawkins coming this way?"

Chapter Sixteen

Meadow chuckled. "Well, he certainly is. It looks as though Hawkins has decided to come speak to *us*."

Beatrice looked past Hawkins to Malcolm to see what his reaction might be to Hawkins approaching Wynona. She was glad to see that he had a smile on his face and that the worried lines around his eyes appeared to be disappearing. Maybe Malcolm thought Wynona could be good for Hawkins.

Beatrice murmured, "We should be going."

"Oh, please don't!" said Wynona quickly. "I'd rather you'd stay here."

Meadow said, "Okay, but if we feel like we're not needed, Beatrice and I are going to scoot out of here!"

Hawkins hesitantly approached them and the ladies stood up.

No one spoke for a couple of seconds, and Meadow, never one for awkward silences, said in a blustery voice, "Hawkins, we're so sorry. But what a lovely service."

But Hawkins only nodded vaguely, his eyes still focused on Wynona. He said, "Wynona, I'm so sorry. For everything. Can you forgive me?"

Wynona nodded and Hawkins's eyes filled with tears. She stepped forward to give him a hug and he clutched her as if she were a life preserver.

Beatrice gave Meadow a meaningful look and they both hurried away.

Meadow said, "I'm so happy for them. Aren't you, Beatrice?"

"I'm tentatively happy," said Beatrice. "I do think they have a lot to work through. And a murder investigation to survive."

Meadow gave her an indulgent smile. "Beatrice. Always the realist." She peered across the cemetery. "Is Malcolm asking us to come over?"

Beatrice started walking. "He sure is."

Meadow said uneasily, "I wonder what he thinks of the Hawkins-Wynona reunion."

"From what I saw a few minutes ago, it looked as though he was delighted that they were together," said Beatrice. "At least, I hope that I was reading it right."

Malcolm looked tired, but gave them both a smile. He gestured over to where Hawkins and Wynona were sitting on the bench. "Am I right in guessing that you ladies had something to do with Wynona being here today?"

Meadow turned bright red and said in a flustered voice, "Oh, I don't know about that. Beatrice? Do you know anything about that?"

Before Beatrice could answer, Malcolm laughed and held up his hands. "It's okay! I was going to thank you for getting her out here. I haven't seen Hawkins look this relaxed and unstressed for months. Wynona is clearly good for him."

Beatrice noticed that Della's lips tightened as if she was biting back an argument. She stared at her nails as if trying to keep out of it.

Beatrice said, "Wynona wanted to come and show her support for the family. Especially Hawkins. I just helped convince her that it was the right thing to do and that no one would be upset that she was here."

Malcolm smiled. "Definitely not upset. I'm delighted that Hawkins is happy. And delighted that this service is over." He rubbed his eyes. "I'm missing about twenty hours of sleep, I think."

He turned and opened his mouth to call to Della when a middle-aged woman came up to Della and gave her a huge hug. Della started to cry and both women walked off to sit on a wooden bench.

Malcolm grimaced. "Looks like I might be here for a while longer. Now I'm not just waiting for Hawkins, I'm waiting for Della, too."

Meadow said sympathetically, "You've got to be absolutely exhausted."

Malcolm nodded. "It's been awful." He hesitated, and then continued as if the murders were at the forefront of his mind and he couldn't really avoid talking about them. "I was at least halfway prepared for my father's death. After all, he was an old man. I wasn't prepared for it to be like *this*," he said with a wave of his hand toward the casket. "But Sadie?" He shook his head.

Beatrice took a deep breath and then pressed, "And you're sure you didn't see anyone?"

"No," he said quickly, "As I told you before, I was exhausted and turned in with Della as soon as supper was finished. Or, rather, *before* supper was finished, since I'd just been picking at my meal."

Meadow managed a look of surprise. "But," she stammered, "I thought someone we'd talked to was sure they saw you out taking a walk a couple of nights ago."

Malcolm flushed in confusion. "Someone on our property? Well, they must have gotten the night wrong."

"I'm afraid not," said Beatrice, sounding apologetic.

Now it was Malcolm's turn to study his hands. "I did go out. Oh, I turned in early, like I said. But I couldn't sleep. All I kept thinking of was my father and how he died. I tossed and turned for a little while until I finally decided to get up and take a walk. That's all."

"You hadn't mentioned that before," said Beatrice softly.

"Only because it didn't seem important," said Malcolm with a slight smile and a shrug of the shoulder. "And Della was sound asleep. I ended up right back in bed."

But there was something about the way he tacked on the bit about Della that made Beatrice wonder.

Meadow's face creased with worry. "Who on earth do you think might be responsible for all this, Malcolm?"

Malcolm spread his hands wide and looked wordlessly at them.

"No idea?" asked Beatrice. "Was anyone upset with Sadie? Had you overheard her arguing with anyone?"

He sighed. "Well, Sadie could get pretty wound up. Sometimes she wasn't the easiest person to get along with. She was impatient, with people in general. I remember being very surprised that she chose to go into social work, considering her short fuse. But apparently, when she was at work, she was incredibly patient and understanding." He laughed, then looked sad, remembering that his sister was now gone. "I guess I haven't gotten used to speaking of her in the past tense. But the point is: had she argued with anyone?"

Beatrice nodded.

Malcolm said, "Well, of course, you saw that she'd argued with Hawkins over Father's funeral arrangements. But that's hardly something you'd murder someone over. And she's argued with me, too. It's been pretty tense around the house lately, as you can imagine."

He looked sad at the thought of having argued with his sister.

Meadow said, "Of *course* it was tense there. I can't even imagine."

"What did you argue about?" asked Beatrice. She glanced over and saw Della and Hawkins were still caught up talking in their respective conversations. She hoped she had enough time to talk to him before they came back over.

"Oh, you know," said Malcolm with a sigh. "We'd just heard from the lawyer about the will." He hesitated, and then said, "Ordinarily, I'd keep my mouth shut about financial things, but somehow it will all end up being common knowledge in Dappled Hills anyway. Father had apparently gotten tired of Hawkins always being low on cash and didn't give him a full-third of his estate. Although I don't think he'll be hurting if he is responsible with what he did leave him. And Father left the estate to Sadie and me."

Beatrice raised her eyebrows. "And you had different ideas for what to do with it?"

Malcolm laughed. "How did you guess? Sadie wanted to sell it. I wanted to keep it up and keep things as they were ... for a while. I also had some ideas of maybe allowing part of the house to function as a bed and breakfast. But Sadie wanted no part of that idea. To her, it was going to be nothing but trouble. All she wanted was to make a few updates to the house and sell it." He shrugged. "We argued over that, sure. But we were hardly at each other's throats."

"And Della?" asked Meadow, as they turned to look at the young woman who was still chatting with her friend out of earshot.

Malcolm said, "Are you kidding? Della and Sadie always got along great. I mean, sometimes Sadie maybe got a little irritated with Della—maybe she wanted to get her to hurry up when we were all about to leave. Della can be a little poky sometimes when she's getting ready. But that's it. They were almost like siblings."

Beatrice found that hard to believe. She'd seen Sadie with Della and Sadie always seemed a bit more than irritated with Della. But it seemed to Beatrice like Sadie was genuinely *trying* to include Della in things. "What about Wynona?" she asked quietly. "Did Sadie and Wynona always get along?"

Malcolm nodded. "Most of the time, sure. They were good friends, after all. But Sadie could end up getting frustrated with Wynona. She told me once that she felt like Wynona was just wasting her time trying to get back together with Hawkins. Sadie thought Wynona should just give up. Said that it was never going to happen because Hawkins was too scared of defying Caspian. Sadie thought that Wynona should just move forward and start looking for someone else to have a relationship with."

Beatrice raised her eyebrows. "And what was your response to that?"

Malcolm sighed. "I didn't agree. And I told Sadie that. In fact, I was surprised by Sadie's point of view. After all, Sadie was the one who ended up returning home to try to mend fences with Father—that's hardly moving on. I mean, she definitely left us and struck out on her own when she got sick of our father. But ultimately, she decided that the estrangement didn't make her happy. She ended up coming back home. It was ironic that she was telling Wynona that she should move on."

Meadow asked anxiously, "On a slightly different subject, what are y'all going to do about Sadie's service? I know you just finished this one. Is there anything that we can do to help with planning or bringing food or anything?"

Malcolm smiled at her. "That's really nice of you. But we're actually not going to do anything for a while. She deserves a real service of her own—not something slapped together in haste right after our father's service. Sadie always said that she wanted to be cremated." He closed his eyes briefly as if trying to control his emotions. He opened them and continued, "Once we receive her ... body ... back from the police, we'll follow through with her wishes. Then we'll have a nice memorial service for her at a later date when we have more time to prepare."

Meadow said stoutly, "I think that's a marvelous idea. And it will be so much more thoughtful that way."

Malcolm nodded. Then he said, "All right, it looks as if Della is wrapping things up. And we'll invite Wynona to come home with us. I'll see you both soon, I hope." He gave them a quick hug and then turned to greet Della's friend who was approaching him.

Minutes later, Meadow was driving Beatrice home.

"Well, that was a very interesting funeral," said Meadow. "And I never expected I'd be saying that. The way the service was originally planned, it sounded like it was going to be a very ordinary funeral."

Beatrice said, "It might have been one of the *happiest* funerals I've ever been to. With Wynona and Hawkins getting together."

Meadow drove briefly off the road as she turned and looked at Beatrice.

"Meadow! The road! I swear, I need to take over the driving," said Beatrice.

"Sorry! Sorry! Just a momentary distraction," said Meadow, hastily jerking the wheel and getting them back on the road again. "I was just thinking: is it *really* a good thing?"

Beatrice said, "Why wouldn't it be? Wynona is terrific for Hawkins. I haven't known the man very long, but this is the first time I've ever seen him that he hasn't looked abjectly miserable."

"Because he *could* be a murderer, Beatrice! Or *she* could be a murderer. We just heard Malcolm tell us that Wynona sometimes argued with Sadie," said Meadow.

"Yes, but that's hardly motive to kill someone. Now, if Sadie had seen something that pointed to Wynona as Caspian's killer, then that might be more of a motive." Beatrice stopped. Wasn't there something Sadie had said? Something that she had seen?

"So she's still in the picture," said Meadow gloomily. "Poor Wynona—never able to find true happiness."

"Well, we're still working on it. These deaths may have nothing to do with Wynona at all," said Beatrice.

"But they could have to do with Hawkins! And what do we know about Hawkins? That he was, as you said, abjectly miserable. That he needed money. That he gambled. That he was furious with his father for depriving him of the woman he loved. That he frequently argued with Caspian."

"And he argued with Sadie, too, even about minor things like Caspian's funeral. But that doesn't necessarily mean he's a killer." Beatrice sighed. "Although I did think it was petty of Caspian to not give Hawkins a share in the estate. I wonder if Hawkins knew that, or if the contents of the will were a total surprise."

Meadow pulled into Beatrice's driveway. "If he *did* know, then he wouldn't have really had a motive for killing Caspian."

"No, he still had a motive—he was angry at his father for forbidding his relationship with Wynona," said Beatrice. She thought for a minute. "I'm still thinking about what Hawkins said. That Sadie was upset that her father had been murdered out of greed."

Meadow nodded. "Well, if you think about it, it makes sense. Sadie wasn't exactly a fan of greedy people. Her own father had been so greedy that he'd stopped supporting her mother, even when she became ill."

"Yes. But how did Sadie *know* that her father was killed because of greed? It sounds as if she knew who his murderer was and the motive, too." Beatrice frowned.

"Then do you think that *Hawkins* knows more than that? Since he was talking to Sadie? Do you think she gave him any clues?" asked Meadow.

"I don't know. But I think I'm going to go over again and talk to him," said Beatrice. "Except that I don't really have a great excuse. And I just saw him."

Meadow said, "You have the perfect excuse to go over there. Quilting. You're over there to see if Della wants some extra fabric that you can't use. After all, you've been rearranging your household and trying to get organized before Wyatt moves in after the wedding. Then you can try and snag a quiet conversation with Hawkins. He's probably out walking the estate, as usual."

"That's true. Although I'm not sure I *do* have some extra fabric. I tend to buy only what I need," said Beatrice.

"That sounds like you. Then you should come by *my* house. I have *gobs* of extra fabric that I don't need that's been collecting over the course of twenty-five years. I'd go with you over there, but I told Ash that I'd go with him to the caterer to help choose a menu for their rehearsal dinner," said Meadow. "We'll just zip by my house and then I'll drop you back home."

Beatrice said, "All right. Although I still feel like it seems a little weird of me to be going by their house on the day of Caspian's funeral. And after having just seen them."

Meadow said, "It's not weird at all! You simply had them on your mind and forgot to mention to Della that you had extra fabric for her when you saw her. You wanted to go ahead and drop it by and ask if there's anything you can do while you're out—something like that. What could be more natural?"

Beatrice wasn't so sure, although she took the extra fabric from Meadow's house, which Meadow stuck in a tote bag. "FYI, Meadow, there isn't just fabric in here. There's a pair of shears, rulers, and batting. You don't need any of this?"

Meadow shrugged. "I have way too much stuff. You've inspired me to clear some things out. I don't need that ancient tote bag, either."

When Meadow dropped Beatrice back home, she decided to go in for at least a little while. She wanted to put her feet up for a bit.

An hour later, Beatrice picked up the large tote bag, and headed off to the Nelms estate.

The sun was starting to set. She parked the car in the circular driveway and got out with the bag of fabric. She hesitated for a minute, looking to see if she could spot Hawkins walking around. But she didn't even see Barkis there.

Beatrice walked up to the front door and rang the doorbell. After a minute, she heard footsteps coming.

Chapter Seventeen

Hawkins opened the door. But instead of the dejected and downbeat Hawkins that usually answered the door, this Hawkins had a cheerful smile and a light in his eye.

He also seemed to be in a very good mood—especially considering that his father's funeral was only hours earlier.

"Beatrice! It's so good to see you." He reached out his hand and shook her free one. "Wynona told me that you'd persuaded her that it would be all right to go to the service today. I'm so glad you did."

"She wanted to come, it's just that she was worried how her presence would be received," said Beatrice.

Hawkins smiled at her and then stepped backwards. "I'm sorry—would you like to come in? Is that something I can carry for you?"

"It's just some fabric that I brought for Della," said Beatrice. "I'm trying to make room in my cottage for Wyatt and his things after the wedding. You wouldn't believe all the clutter I'd collected. I thought maybe Della could use this fabric since she's starting out with quilting."

She walked in behind Hawkins and he gestured to a chair in the drawing room. Beatrice shook her head and said quickly, "I really shouldn't stay. I know it's been a really rough day for the whole family. As I said, I just wanted to drop these things off for Della. And ... well, I wanted to ask you about something. There was one thing you said that I can't seem to get out of my mind."

Hawkins raised his eyebrows. "Sure—if I can help you."

"You said that Sadie mentioned that she was sad that your father was murdered for the wrong reasons. Do you know what she meant by that or if she somehow knew who was responsible for your father's death?" asked Beatrice.

Hawkins looked surprised and then thoughtful. "You know, it may sound crazy, but I haven't even spent time thinking that over. Obviously, *something* about it stuck in my head for me to mention it to you.

Sadie seemed to think that Father was killed for money. And that *does* make it seem like she knew who was behind it. But she didn't tell me." A look of frustration crossed his face. "If I hadn't been so caught up in my own problems, I'd have asked her right then for an explanation. But I feel as though I might barely have been listening to her. That makes me feel terrible now, saying that."

Beatrice said quietly, "But you didn't know she'd be gone when you were having that conversation with her."

"No. No, I didn't. Which just serves as a reminder that I need to treasure conversations with *everyone* since we never know how long a person has left." Now Hawkins looked slightly abashed. "Sorry. That's kind of a downer of a thing to say, I guess. Maybe the funeral had that effect on me today. But listen—you weren't here to talk with me and I was on my way out the door. Wynona said she'd like me to join her when she walks her dog." He flushed with pleasure. "I know Della's around here somewhere, although Malcolm is out. Let me give her a call."

He did and a minute later Della peered out from the top of the steep stone staircase. She smiled when she saw Beatrice.

"Well, hello there!" she said perkily. "Good to see you again today."

"See you soon, Beatrice," said Hawkins with a quick grin as he hurried out the door.

"I know you must be surprised to see me again today," said Beatrice. "But I've been clearing out my house in preparation for Wyatt's moving in, and I wanted to see if you could use these fabrics that I don't need." She held up the tote bag.

Della's cheeks dimpled. "Beatrice, that's so sweet of you! I was thinking that I'd try to get involved in Village Quilters after all. In memory of Sadie, you know. She was planning on being part of your guild and I thought it might be a nice way to honor her. The fabrics will be perfect."

Della started to walk down the stairs and Beatrice said quickly, "Don't worry about coming down—I don't want to interrupt whatever it is that you were doing. I can just leave them here at the bottom of the stairs."

Della said, "That would be great." Then she paused. "You know, I just thought of something you might be interested in seeing. I wasn't part of the whole tour that Sadie gave you—did she show you the historical quilt the family has?"

Beatrice considered this. "Sadie pointed out a few quilts, but she didn't especially indicate that one was more special than the others."

"You'd love this one. They have it hanging in a sitting room up here and it must be at least one hundred and fifty years old. I'm scared to touch it, but if you'd like to see it?"

Beatrice bit back a sigh. She really wanted to head back home and have a nice, simple dinner and a phone call to Wyatt. But it sounded as though she could be spending a lot of extra time with Della, since she was planning on joining the guild. It might do Beatrice good to try and reach out more.

"That would be great," she said in as peppy a voice as she could muster. She headed up the stairs thinking that at least she was getting her exercise on the staircase. With all the celebration dinners, she'd felt a little celebration weight getting added.

Della paused as Beatrice reached the top landing. "You were having quite the conversation with Hawkins, weren't you? Doesn't he seem so much better than he was earlier?"

"He's vastly improved, I thought. But then, Wynona seems to have that effect on him," said Beatrice mildly. She still held the bag of fabric and she reached out toward Della. "Here's the fabric, by the way. I think you'll have better use for it than I will."

But Della didn't seem to want to talk about the fabric and didn't seem inclined to take it. "You know, the acoustics at the front of the house are a funny thing. You can hear every word someone says at the front door upstairs. That's something to do with all the marble and granite, I think. Stone has a way of helping voices to carry."

Beatrice felt a cold shiver go up her spine. "Our conversation was fairly innocuous, Della. Although maybe you didn't find it so."

"You ask a lot of questions," said Della with a smirking smile. "Too many questions, I think. It would probably be best if you just let the family be. There's lots of grieving to get through for both Malcolm and Hawkins."

Beatrice backed slowly away. The mention of Malcolm made her think about Malcolm's alibi being blown. If Malcolm hadn't been sleeping and had left the house, then he couldn't be *Della's* alibi, either. And that particular thought made her reach surreptitiously in the tote bag until her hand grabbed the shears.

"Where's Malcolm?" asked Beatrice, a little breathlessly.

"Out. He's taking care of estate business," said Della.

"Which is a good thing, since you're about to be very wealthy," said Beatrice flatly.

"Exactly," said Della with a simpering smile.

Beatrice backed up until she could feel part of the bannister bump against her back. "It's a funny thing about Malcolm's alibi."

"What's that?" asked Della, raising her eyebrows.

"Well, it wasn't true. At least, his story wasn't *exactly* true. He neglected the part where he couldn't sleep and decided to go for a walk. A walk that likely intersected with Sadie's walk," said Beatrice.

Della's face closed down, the perkiness and even the simpering gone now. "Malcolm would never hurt Sadie."

"No, I have the feeling that he wouldn't. He was a devoted brother to her. But *you* were devoted to Malcolm. You'd have done anything for him—and for the money that he was going to inherit. And if Malcolm's alibi was wrecked by the fact that someone saw him out on the grounds, then *your* alibi was also wrecked. Because Malcolm was your alibi and you were his," said Beatrice.

Della's eyes flashed with anger. "See? All you do is nose around. You should learn how to mind your own business. You've got a wedding to plan. The last thing you should be doing is getting involved in things like this."

"Like what? Murder? Let me guess how this all started. Actually, I don't really have to guess, do I? Sadie knew how it started. She wasn't exactly her father's biggest fan, but she was upset because she thought that his death was motivated by greed. She spent the final year of her life trying to make things right with her father—even though it sounded as though Sadie wasn't at fault for their estrangement. And she knew something. She knew who murdered her father and why, didn't she?"

Della shrugged a shoulder languidly, but her eyes were locked on Beatrice's.

"And you knew that Sadie knew," said Beatrice finally.

Della gave a short laugh. "I can promise you that Sadie said *nothing* to me about it. Would she seriously have taken me to your bridal shower if she'd thought I'd killed her father?"

"I think she must have only suspected your involvement then. But something made her realize it must have been you. You seem like you're always lurking around, for one thing," said Beatrice.

Della snorted. "That's ironic for *you* to say."

"That day that we were trying to help you plan Caspian's funeral, for instance. You were outside the room quite a bit, but I bet you knew a lot about what was said. You were getting drinks and snacks together, but you were also listening. And that was the day that Sadie mentioned something about having a strong suspicion about who might be responsible. You could also have heard Sadie tell Hawkins that she knew the motive for the murder. You most *certainly* heard Hawkins repeat what Sadie said when he was speaking to me a few minutes ago," said Beatrice.

"What does my 'lurking around', as you call it, have to do with Caspian's death?" asked Della, sounding bored. She took another, rather menacing, step toward Beatrice.

"You're very good at being out of sight. Good at listening in. Basically, you're good at being sneaky. Which is the perfect trait for quickly getting rid of Caspian. Because he was starting to turn on you, wasn't he, Della? Did he sense that greediness that Sadie was talking about? At any rate, whether he was trying to influence Malcolm to break up with you, or whether you simply were ready for Malcolm to receive his inheritance, you were ready to get rid of him. It was probably pretty easy to slip the pills into Caspian's drink. Sometimes the drink was unattended and sometimes you helped to make the drink, yourself. I suspect, while Malcolm was getting ready, you slipped away. You listened as our little tour of the house, led by Sadie, went by. When the coast was clear, you slipped in Caspian's room, picked up a pillow, and smothered him while he slept."

Della was silent, eyes steely.

Beatrice took a deep breath and continued. "Sadie must have realized you did it. Maybe because she couldn't picture either of her brothers as a killer—or her best friend. So you needed to get rid of Sadie, too."

Della rolled her eyes. "I turned in early the night Sadie died."

"Maybe you did. But I think that you watched *Malcolm* turn in early. Then you headed out after Sadie. Barkis has been doing a lot of landscaping lately and it was easy enough to find a weapon—there was a wheelbarrow full of paving bricks right there. Maybe you even had a conversation with Sadie before you struck her," said Beatrice.

Something seemed to snap in Della then. "Maybe I didn't. Maybe Sadie never saw what was coming."

"And then you shoved her off the dock into the water. Just to be sure she was dead," said Beatrice sharply.

"I'm never one to leave a job halfway finished," said Della.

Beatrice said, "I thought that when Malcolm was wandering around that he must have seen Sadie's body. That maybe he was too worried about how it would look if he was the one to have discovered her and so he didn't report it. But now I'm thinking he never *did* see Sadie. That it was just as he said—that he couldn't sleep after supper and he decided to take a walk. Maybe he even saw Sadie on his walk ... when she was still alive. But the property here is large and he kept on walking. I'm thinking that he saw *you* when he was wrapping up his walk, Della. Even though you'd turned in early."

Della said, "I was almost to the house when he saw me."

"And Malcolm didn't know that you'd just murdered his sister, did he? Because he didn't see the body. But you must have given him an excuse for what you were doing outside," said Beatrice.

"I told him that I was looking for him, of course," said Della with a shrug. "That I'd woken up and didn't see him there. I got up to look for him."

"And then, the next morning, Hawkins found Sadie's body. Surely, Malcolm must have wondered if you had something to do with it, Della."

Della snorted. "Love is blind, remember? He was more concerned about the fact that he'd been outside during the time she was likely murdered. He was concerned about *his* alibi. He didn't even question me when I told him that I was only out for a second and out looking for him."

"It sounds like he was still holding out hope that you weren't involved," said Beatrice. "What's he going to think when he knows that you were responsible for both his father's death and his sister's?"

"He's not going to *think* anything, because he's not going to *know* about it," hissed Della. She lunged at Beatrice, but Beatrice was ready. She gripped the shears in her right hand and threw the large tote bag with her left hand.

Chapter Eighteen

The bag hit Della's legs and she stumbled, sliding on the fabric on the stone floor at the top of the stairs. She clutched wildly for the banister, but it only served to give her more momentum down the stairs. She was able to come to a crashing halt at the first landing, however, precariously holding on to the stone stair.

Beatrice ran down the stairs as fast as she could go, being careful not to tumble down them, herself. Della gave a snarling gasp as Beatrice passed her, snatching at her legs but getting only air.

By the time she'd reached the bottom of the stairs, though, Beatrice realized that Della was after her. What's more, Della was quite a bit younger than she was. Beatrice sped up, panting, fumbling for her car keys in the pocket of her khaki capris.

Beatrice was nearly to her car when Della sped up and launched herself at Beatrice's back with a wild cry, knocking the breath out of her.

Beatrice turned as much as she could under Della's weight and jabbed the shears into Della's side. Della hissed and backed off for a second.

Beatrice was about to try to wriggle free when she heard an icy voice splitting through the silence.

"Della, what on *earth* are you doing?"

It was Malcolm, and Beatrice had never been happier to hear another human being's voice in her life.

Della seemed to melt. Her body went limp and Beatrice scrambled up, pushing Della off of her as she got to her feet. Della, looking warily at Malcolm, slowly rose to her feet, as well.

"Malcolm, you don't understand. I was doing it for us!" Della's eyes were pleading. "Let me just ... finish. I'll put her at the bottom of the stairs and it will appear she's tumbled. No one has to know! It's better this way, believe me. Then we'll have such a great life together. I'll make you so happy." She reached out a shaking hand to him.

Malcolm pushed it away.

"I don't know exactly what you were doing, but I can take a guess. Suddenly, everything has become very clear to me," he said coldly.

"Malcolm, I can tell that you're angry. Of course you're angry," spluttered Della. "But you'll understand when I explain it to you. I never did anything for *myself*. It was all about *us*, always."

"No, that's where you're wrong, Della. It was about *you*. Only you. You wanted to marry me because you saw dollar signs. You knew I was going to inherit Father's money and you simply couldn't wait, could you?" Malcolm sounded very detached, almost clinical, as he spoke to Della.

He turned to Beatrice. "You had a lucky escape. But you've also helped *me* have a lucky escape. Can you imagine, being married to a murderer? Father knew what he was talking about. He was starting to turn against Della, right before he died. I wonder if that had something to do with the timing of it all ... his death."

Della stared at him. "We were going to be happy," she repeated. Then she grabbed Malcolm's hand, which lay limply in hers. "No one has to know about this. Right? Beatrice, I'm sorry ... you'll accept my apology, won't you? Can't we just keep going as we were before, Malcolm?"

But Beatrice was already phoning Ramsay. The siren, just a few minutes later, broke into the tense silence.

Ramsay waited until the state police had taken Della away before asking Malcolm or Beatrice for their accounts. He did quickly phone Wyatt, who joined her in just minutes looking white-faced and shaken—until he saw with his own eyes that Beatrice was all right. He wordlessly took her in his arms and held her until she felt the stress melt away. Then they sat next to each other in the Nelms's yard furniture, holding hands.

Ramsay spoke with Malcolm first. Malcolm hadn't fallen apart as Hawkins had, but his usual confidence was gone and he looked more uncertain than Beatrice had ever seen him. It looked as if he'd had the rug yanked out from under him.

Ramsay finally came over to speak with Beatrice. He said grimly, "Malcolm confirmed that you were attacked and that Della had implicitly admitted to everything. I'm glad he did because otherwise, it would have been your word against Della's."

Beatrice said with a sigh, "And I know it makes it look like I was courting trouble by coming over here. But until one point in the visit, I didn't realize that Della was the villain of the story. I'd come over to ask Hawkins about an offhanded remark he'd made about Sadie: that she was angry that their father had been murdered over money."

Wyatt said quietly, "Which would have meant that Sadie had some idea who was behind his murder."

"Exactly," said Beatrice. "But Hawkins was about to run out the door to see Wynona—he still hasn't returned, I guess. Malcolm was out and so Della was the only one home. She wanted to show me some sort of vintage quilt that she thought I might not have seen during the original tour of the house." It seemed very important to Beatrice that neither Ramsay nor Wyatt thought she'd been reckless during her ill-fated visit to the Nelms house.

Ramsay nodded. He took a few notes. "And, clearly, at some point, things changed."

"That's right. Della was furious about how 'nosy' I was being. And she kept moving closer in a rather threatening manner. It was a good thing that Meadow had loaded that tote bag up with all kinds of quilting supplies—the shears came in handy." Beatrice shivered.

Ramsay said, "So money was the motivating factor. Della was ready for Malcolm to receive his inheritance."

"That's part of it, yes. And I suppose Della knew that Hawkins, despite being the eldest child, wasn't going to be receiving the lion's share of the money since Caspian was so irritated already about loaning him money. Della knew that Malcolm would be receiving a good chunk of the estate. But that wasn't the only reason," said Beatrice.

Wyatt said in a thoughtful voice, "Was Caspian also turning against Della, as he'd turned against Wynona, earlier?"

Beatrice nodded. "That's right. Apparently, he wasn't liking what he saw in Della, or maybe Della's true colors were showing the more time Caspian spent with her. Either way, he was starting to show his disapproval more frequently. Della was desperate to continue the relationship."

"But Sadie and Della were friends," said Ramsay. "Was greed the motivating factor in her death, too? With Sadie out of the way, the rest of the estate would have been divided up between Hawkins and Malcolm."

"Maybe that was part of it, again. But I think the real problem was that Sadie either knew or had somehow figured out that Della was responsible for Caspian's death. And she clearly wasn't going to stay quiet about it. She hated the problems that money caused in a family—it was the main reason she'd become estranged from her father ... he'd withheld needed money from Sadie's mother. The more Sadie thought about it, the more aggravated she'd become. Della must have been worried that Sadie was going to say something to Malcolm about her suspicions. She decided to ensure that wasn't going to happen," said Beatrice.

Ramsay sighed, "And Della had the extra incentive of the money, on top of it. For her, it must not have been a difficult decision to make."

Beatrice said, "I didn't think that Della and Sadie were all that close, anyway. I think, in some ways, that they each resented the other."

Beatrice suddenly felt very tired. And a little sore on top of it all. Wyatt gave her hand a reassuring squeeze. "Is it all right if I take Beatrice back home now?"

Ramsay peered closer at Beatrice. "Of course! You look completely tapped out, Beatrice. Go home and rest. You probably could have used the rest even *before* someone made an attempt on your life today. When's the big day? Coming up quickly, right?"

"A week from Saturday," said Beatrice with a smile at Wyatt. "I'm pretty sure I'll be recovered by then."

"Well, one thing I can promise you," said Ramsay fervently. "There won't be any more crime in Dappled Hills to investigate in the interim. Not if I have to patrol the streets day and night. We'll have a crime-free period in Dappled Hills, and you'll focus only on the wedding!"

Chapter Nineteen

And that's exactly the way it went. The citizens of the small town of Dappled Hills were as good as gold. Beatrice had a lovely bridesmaid luncheon with Piper, her only attendant, at their favorite restaurant downtown (they both ordered heaping bowls of shrimp and grits and white wine) several days before the wedding.

The night before the wedding, Beatrice and Wyatt went out to dinner at their favorite restaurant in Dappled Hills. Beatrice gave a sigh of contentment as she looked across the candlelit table at Wyatt. He reached over and squeezed her hand. "Happy?" he asked.

She nodded with a smile.

He let go of her hand and stooped to pick up something out of a bag beside him. "I have something for you," he said. He smiled tentatively at her.

Beatrice tilted her head inquisitively as he handed her a rectangular white box wrapped tightly with a white ribbon. She opened the box slowly and then beamed at him. "A painting!"

Beatrice held the painting in the light from the candle. It wasn't just a painting, it was a landscape of a place that was meaningful to them both—the waterfalls at their favorite picnic spot.

Wyatt asked hesitantly, "What do you think?"

Beatrice gave the painting a quick appraisal and then smiled at Wyatt. "It's lovely. Oh, it's unschooled and perhaps a bit undisciplined, but that's easily fixed with some direction. But Wyatt, it's absolutely beautiful. I love the way your painting doesn't just capture the scenery, but the real fell and emotion from the place. And I especially love that you've given it to me."

Wyatt gave her a relieved grin. "I wanted you to have it. You always said you feel more alive there. I thought it might be a good way to help you feel more alive every day, not just the ones when we can escape for a hike."

"It's perfect. And it's all right if I hang it in our house?"

He made a small grimace and then slowly nodded.

"That's good. Because, you know, I'm not running a museum anymore. If I'm happy to put my own imperfect quilts out for display, I'd love putting your own, excellent, paintings out, too.

Wyatt reached out his hand for hers again and then next few minutes they were just quietly happy together.

The next morning was their wedding day; a sunny morning with wispy clouds punctuating a brilliantly blue sky. Piper helped her mother put on her wedding dress. Piper said, "Mama, you look beautiful!"

Beatrice thought that maybe beautiful was a relative term, but she agreed that she looked as beautiful as it was possible for her to look. The dress was a dark gray sheath with a delicate lace overlay, a round neckline, and a sheer yoke in the front and back. The dress set off the platinum-white of her hair in a flattering way.

"Thanks, Piper. And you look stunning," said Beatrice. Piper wore a simple, black sheath dress and wore her hair up.

Piper gave her a hug. "Let's use June Bug's handkerchief as the bouquet wrap."

Piper carefully placed the handkerchief over the wrapped stems of the gardenias in Beatrice's simple, but fragrant bouquet.

As Beatrice walked down the short aisle to where Wyatt stood next to his best man James, she saw the smiling faces of her best friends (both Posy's and Meadow's faces a bit weepy and Harper brushing away a stray tear), and the love and pride in Wyatt's eyes as she joined him at the front of the chapel.

The minister smiled at them both and softly started the ceremony that would join them together, surrounded by the people who loved them.

Wyatt gave Beatrice a tender kiss at the end of the ceremony to start their life together.

Meadow and Piper had insisted on transforming the small church dining hall. They'd lovingly hung beautiful quilts and the Village Quilters had collaborated on stringing the hall with cheerful fairy lights to give it an intimate feel. White tablecloths covered round tables. And the food was Southern cooking at its best.

June Bug's niece, Katy, shyly helped with the guest book, proud to be playing a role in such a big day. She spoke quietly to each guest as they came up.

June Bug beamed at Beatrice. "Scooter has been so good for her! She's opening up more and more."

Beatrice gave her a quick hug. "Pets can work wonders, can't they?"

It was a lovely, simple, happy reception. But just the same, Beatrice was glad when it was time to leave with Wyatt for their short honeymoon at a mountain resort in Asheville, North Carolina.

When they returned from the honeymoon, and were walking down the walkway to Beatrice's cottage, Wyatt looked at her and said gently, "You know that it might take us a little while to completely settle in. There's no rush. We can take our time. It looks like your brain is whirring, thinking of all the things you need to do."

Beatrice smiled at him. "You know me well. I'll try not to overdo it. Although we do need to pick up Noo-noo from Meadow and Ramsay. I'm sure she's ready to escape from Boris the dog at this point. And I've really missed her." She squinted at her front porch. "What's that?"

It was a white box wrapped in a white ribbon. There was a robin's egg blue tag on it. Beatrice peered at it. "It's a gift from Meadow."

They brought it inside and sat down together on the sofa. Beatrice unwrapped the present and took the lid off the box. She lifted out a quilted album and suddenly felt her eyes mist up. "Meadow," she said with a smile and a shake of her head.

Wyatt put his arm around her. "What does the note inside say?"

Beatrice picked up the small note inside, written in Meadow's loopy script. "It says: 'to help you remember the blur.'"

She opened up the album and saw it all there—their engagement, their wedding, and their reception. All the moments she'd worried she'd forget in the bustle and hurry leading up to the wedding. "How was she able to sneak in so much picture taking?" asked Beatrice.

Wyatt smiled. "She must have worked very hard on the furtive photography. Look, she's even included a photo of you and Piper at your bridesmaid luncheon."

Beatrice said, "And Piper is smiling right at the camera! She must have known about Meadow's project. I'll have to run over and thank her … and pick up our sweet Noo-noo."

"I'll cook us something really quickly while you do," said Wyatt, rising from the sofa.

And their first evening of their new life at home was spent eating breakfast for supper and reliving their wedding, Noo-noo happily at their feet, leaning into each other as they looked through the pictures and remembered.

About the Author

Elizabeth writes the Southern Quilting mysteries and Memphis Barbeque mysteries for Penguin Random House and the Myrtle Clover series for Midnight Ink and independently. She blogs at ElizabethSpannCraig.com/blog, named by Writer's Digest as one of the 101 Best Websites for Writers. Elizabeth makes her home in Matthews, North Carolina, with her husband and two teenage children.

Sign up for Elizabeth's free newsletter to stay updated on its release: http://eepurl.com/kCy5j

Find Elizabeth:

On Facebook elizabethspanncraig/

Twitter https://twitter.com/elizabethscraig

Her website: http://elizabethspanncraig.com/

Email her at elizabethspanncraig@gmail.com

This and That

I love hearing from my readers. You can find me on Facebook as Elizabeth Spann Craig Author, on Twitter as elizabethscraig, on my website at elizabethspanncraig.com, and by email at elizabethspanncraig@gmail.com. Thanks so much for reading my book...I appreciate it. If you enjoyed the story, would you please leave a short review on the site where you purchased it? Just a few words would be great. Not only do I feel encouraged reading them, but they also help other readers discover my books. Thank you!

Interested in having a character named after you? In a Myrtle Clover tote bag? Or even just your name listed in the acknowledgments of a future book? Visit my Patreon page at https://www.patreon.com/elizabethspanncraig .

If you'd like an autographed book for yourself or a friend, please visit my Etsy page: https://www.etsy.com/shop/CozyMysteries

I'd also like to thank some folks who helped me put this book together. Thanks to Amanda Arrieta and Dan Harris for beta reading the story and their helpful suggestions. Thanks to my mother, Beth Spann, for her tireless encouragement and help. Thanks to Judy Beatty for editing the book and making it better. Thanks again to Karri Klawiter for another wonderful cover. And thanks, as always, to my readers.

Other Works by the Author:

Myrtle Clover Series in Order (be sure to look for the Myrtle series in audio, ebook, and print):
   Pretty is as Pretty Dies
   Progressive Dinner Deadly
   A Dyeing Shame
   A Body in the Backyard
   Death at a Drop-In
   A Body at Book Club
   Death Pays a Visit
   A Body at Bunco
   Murder on Opening Night
   Cruising for Murder
   Cooking is Murder
   Southern Quilting Mysteries in Order:
   Quilt or Innocence
   Knot What it Seams
   Quilt Trip
   Shear Trouble
   Tying the Knot
   Patch of Trouble
   Fall to Pieces
   Pressed for Time (2017)
   Memphis Barbeque Mysteries in Order (Written as Riley Adams):
   Delicious and Suspicious
   Finger Lickin' Dead
   Hickory Smoked Homicide
   Rubbed Out
   And a standalone "cozy zombie" novel: Race to Refuge, written as Liz Craig

Printed in Great Britain
by Amazon